Survival Pod:

Issue One

C. David Apgar

Survival Pod Publishing

Dedication

As writers, this page is our one moment to put into print how much we appreciate everything that those around us have sacrificed in order for us to live our life the way it is supposed to be.

Hence, the dedication page becomes the most difficult of all the pages in a book to write because we never want to leave anyone out.

To my family goes the greatest glory. Father, mother, sister siblings, life partner, and most beloved children. You are the bedrock on which I have built my entire universe.

Like the "Doctor" would say, life is a wibbley-wobbly ball of extraordinary experiences and I have been blessed to have such an eclectic group of individuals to bounce around the planet with.

To Everyone Else: Be you friends, enemies, lovers, liars, a partners in crime or an angel hidden in the shadows... All I can say is thank you. It is in all of you that my stories find the breath of life and immortality amongst the dusty tomes.

“Angels”of the Net”

Producing a book is hard.

There are a million things that go in to it that one never thinks about when beginning a project like this and the largest obstacle by far was the cost.

I'm not a rich man. Not even close. In fact, I'd say I am a lot closer to being dirt poor than I would like to admit most days.

If not for the invaluable support of the following individuals, this entire project would have ground to a halt when it came to the editorial process.

So I raise my goblet high to you, my “Angels of the Web”:

Megan and Christopher Lester

Debra Jean Whitaker

Mary Ann Fitzpatrick

Maggie Macpherson

Eric Damon Walters

Jody Montgomery

Charity Whitaker

Jim Temrowski

Eleanor Howell

John Whitaker

Jessica Apgar

Scott Heenan

David Apgar

Barb Trivett

Michael Lee

Barb Abney

Tina Burgin

Karl Atwerk

AUTHO RISED
51 23
PERSO NNEL
ON LY

5123

Listen close laddie... There are certain places on a starship that a person just doesn't wander into.

Now, any sailor worth his salt knows you stay in your area of concern. What good is a gunner gonna' do down in the guts with a gaggle of reactor brats?

No, no, no.... I'm talking about a place locked away deep in the guts of every battle-wagon and space freighter floating in the black.

An area that's very mention will curl the toes of a battle hardened Marine if spoken of at the wrong time.

On the Maxamillian that place is room 5123. And behind the doors of 5123 there lives a grizzled old man.

A beaten, and weary workman who despite his disheveled appearance and frightening reputation who started out fresh as fish, just like you.

It was in the dark confines of the galley during my first day on the Max that I made his acquaintance.

My nerves were raw from a twelve hour shift at the helm; eyes bloodshot and hands stiff from creeping through a sea of rock and metal that desperately wanted to reach out and caress the Max.

Grabbing a steel tray full of grub from the line in the mess hall, I took a seat at the nearest table and tore into the greasy fare before an acrid smell drew my attention up from the greasy plate of cold corned beef hash.

The rancid tang of melted plastic and burnt syth-oil bit at the back of the throat, causing me to stop eating my meal and casually look about in an attempt to identify the source of the malodorous scent.

And there his sat, obscured by the shadows, sipping on a beat up mug of coffee with his back to the wall.

A rugged, spindly looking man; his red hair having gone white from time and burdens, shone almost yellow beneath the florescent lights.

Here and there you could still pick out the ginger of his youth but the only real color left on his craggy face was in his beard. His hair, wiry like iron shavings, had turned a meandering shade of brown from the chewed up cigar constantly clutched between his teeth.

That night he hung over an ancient, chipped, porcelain mug full o' joe; his back was permanently bent and aching from decades of pulling and straining while crouched over a workbench.

The skin on his rail thin frame seemed to be stretched taunt like flesh across a diamond; the muscles beneath molded from a lifetime at the forge.

Hands of steel, scarred and calloused but still strong as a vice slowly stirring the murky dark liquid in his cup with a bent spoon. These were all the trophies of his trade.

Precious gifts from a lifetime of prying, pulling, and grinding; sometimes working for days to get through a single layer of nano-carbon fiber reinforced with titanium infused steel.

The master of 5123 was used to the idea of tirelessly working for weeks to separate the last pieces of some poor idiot from Winnetka or Minneapolis out of his beloved equipment.

With dark eyes used to looking for the smallest of flaw, he noticed my gaze before I could look away. For long moment I was locked in place by his cold stare before removing the stubby cigar from his lips to speak.

That voice; a haunting, rumbling southern baritone from deep down inside asked, “Did you ever wonder how often the unfortunate meet their maker on a tour out to the rim?”

Not knowing what to say, I just stared back blankly; hoping my lack of response might actually kill the conversation. This was not to be, as he just stared back and continued on.

"Never ignore death, boy. It happens every day on these massive ships. Heart attacks, strokes, faulty oxygen regulators, inversed E.V.A. suit pressure indicators. From full on fuck ups to purely mechanical failures... all these things kill just as easily in space as they do planetside.

Sipping at the cooling coffee, he kept a firm lock on my gaze, "Add in the fools whose brains have turned to mush.

"Those that flush themselves out of an airlock just to make the ceaseless black stop, and the body count adds up real quick on a tour.

"To their credit, at least they are gone forever. Their bodies pick up momentum easily as time and the cold vacuum of the Big Black turning their flesh into icy meteorites.

"A lost soul waiting patiently for the loving grip of gravity and burning embrace of friction to release their energy back into the universe.

"I've seen it play out a thousand ways, nothing surprises me anymore. So believe me when I assure you of this fact Laddie.

"If you don't die peacefully in your bunk, you will probably end up with me down in 5123."

And with that he was done, sucking down the last sips of coffee in his mug before returning to his private domain on the Max.

As my first tour dragged on, his story crawled deep into my mind, taking root in my imagination. It wasn't long before I became obsessed with the murky, somber world hidden behind the dull chrome doors and frosted windows of 5123.

As innocuous as the hundreds of other doors on Maxamillian. There was no great sigil of warning or frighting music to scare away the unknowing or unwary.

To the uneducated, it was just a run of the mill equipment room with a variety of grav tables and dozens of different colored tool boxes lining the walls.

Here and there lay a set of magnetic boots or the occasional helmet with a cracked solar shield. A broken rebreather unit lying in pieces on a dirty workbench; waiting patiently for the master to return and put it back together.

There is nothing terrifying about 5123 until you really think about it and make the connection.

This is no ordinary equipment room.

This is the place where tools go after they kill someone.

Every inoffensive looking, common place piece of equipment laying about 5123 was there because it had failed its human counterpart.

The things that the Big Black will do to a man when the tools built to protect him fail is horrifying.

The vacuum of space can rend flesh like paper, freeze every trace of liquid, cook organs like a Christmas goose in a microwave.

Imagine having your body mass increase to five times its original volume, crushed in your own suit like a human whale because a gauge or valve stopped working correctly.

If this is your fate, 5123 is your destination.

In here your bloated, distended body will be slung up on the grav-tables like a slab of meat waiting to be butchered. The flesh will pour free of the remnants of your E.V.A suit as he cracks it open. Muscle and bone sacrificed to the saw, cut to pieces in order to detach you from the equipment designed to protect it.

The sight of your meat will not stop the banging of his power hammer or silence his gravely voice from grumbling out in frustration at having to clean you from the machines.

Chomping a cigar tightly between clenched teeth, his place is not to mourn for you.

He is to clean the flesh from the machine.

Med teams will come collect what is left, when he is through but the machines are his only real concern.

To him, the mecha is infinitely more complex and diverse than the organics he pressure washes from their systems. It is his responsibility to find out why a tool failed, not to care about the damage it caused to meat.

So pay heed and know this ultimate truth, laddie...

The longer you dance with the dark lady, the more likely pieces of you will end up behind door 5123.

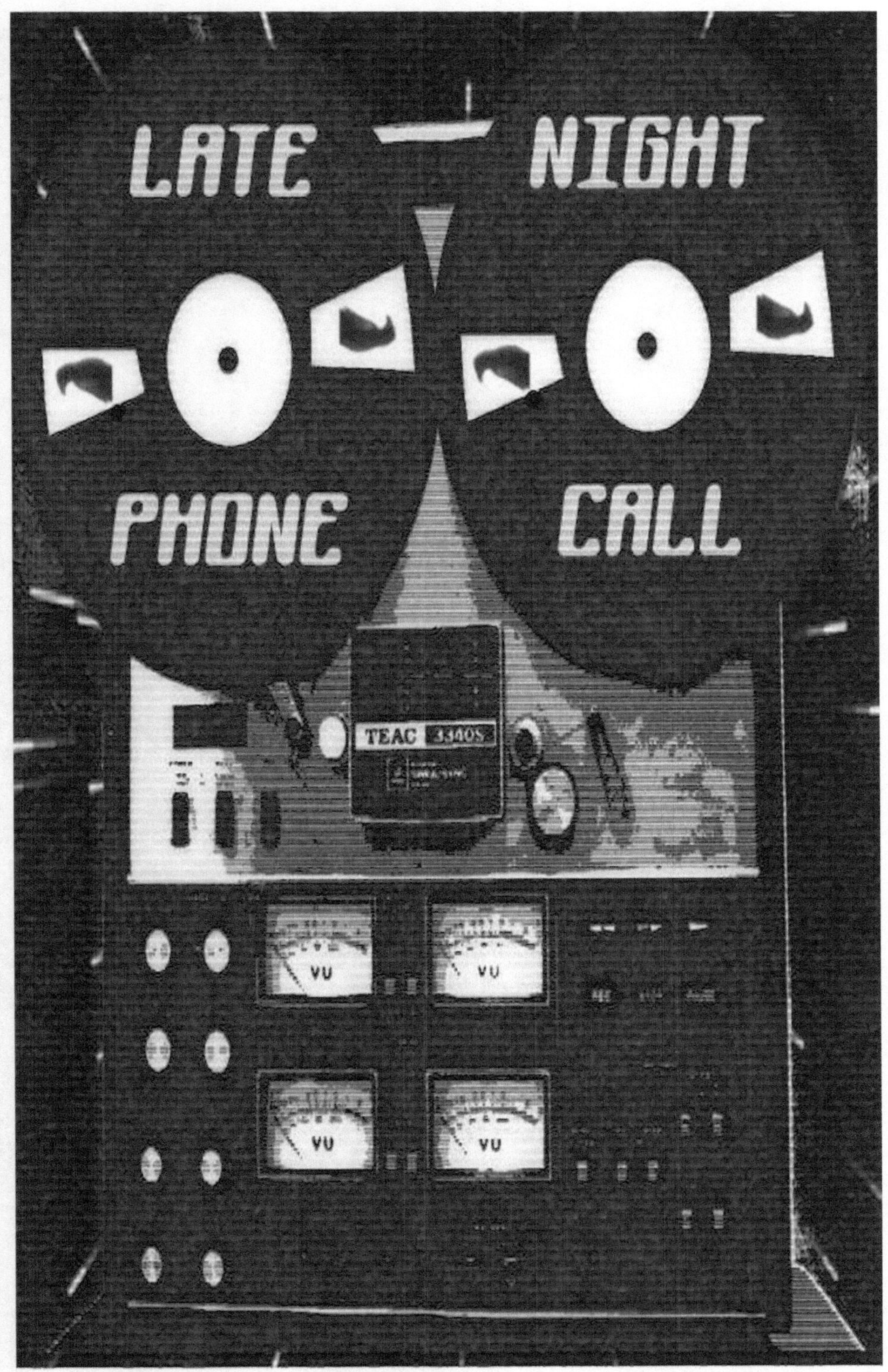
LATE - NIGHT
PHONE CALL
TEAC 3340S
VU
VU
VU
VU

Late Night Phone Call

Barely seventeen, nature had put Alan Short at a disadvantage to say the least.

All gangly arms and uncoordinated feet, his awkward physical appearance was only overshadowed by his stumbling social skills. Alan was a geek in any hallway, in any school in America. And he was perfectly fine with that.

Growing up in the swampy borderland tracts of southeast Texas, Alan didn't fit the traditional Texas teen mold. He would never be that quintessential good ol' boy with a bad attitude & the machismo to back it up. And that was okay too.

Why waste all that time sweating outside? Where was the joy in getting eaten alive by anything with wings? Weren't there enough interesting things at the tip of one's fingers on the Internet to explore?

It were these choices that left Alan with an enormous amount of time invested in subjects as varied as video games to conspiracy theories. If the planet were to fall to a race of unforgiving chimera or shadow government, he had formulated a plan.

On most Saturday nights, Alan could be found in his room, finishing off plates of smoked brisket or BBQ while attached to some form of controller or keyboard.

Despite his skin and bones appearance, Alan actually ate like a shark. If he was moving, it was sure sign he was looking for something to eat. On the weekends, when Mom would take off for fun in Louisiana, he could and regularly would, consume anything she left in the fridge.

Rinsing it all down with a seemingly endless fountain of sugar and taurine powered energy drinks, Alan actually felt pride in his ability to out consume his friends while competeing for digital achievements online via Xbox live.

This Saturday; unlike most, his beloved game console sat cool and quiet all because of aural mysteries of*The Kingdom of the Night* and its amiable host, Artemis Belliard.

Recently, while checking out a story he had seen on the **Science Channel**, Alan came across the *Kingdom* by pure chance.

A random wikihole link on a website filled with targeted ads for gold sellers and "bugout" bags; the *Kingdom* promised a vision into the unknown with just one click.

That was all it took, just one click. One click and he was "through the looking glass."

Ever day; once free of the daily drudgery of the class room, Alan would rush home to listen in to the archival broadcasts stored on its website.

The *Kingdom* was like opening an ark of ancient recordings bearing the secrets of the world, the reel to reel hiss in the background of most of the recordings adding gravitas to the words.

To Alan it didn't matter that some of the broadcasts were two or three decades old, the stories hidden within riveting, real hard-core, black ops, top drawer treasure.

Stories so drenched in government scandals and wet work that it was virtually impossible for a teenager to even think about turning it off.

From remote viewing, the Philadelphia experiment, & Area 51 to MK Ultra, Mothman, or Amityville, Artemis Belliard ran the gambit reporting on stuff that would make Ray Stanz pop a boner in his *Ghostbusters* overalls.

Shows like *Kingdom of the Night,* with their wide-open talk show format, would eventually become the foundation for almost every crazy, "supernatural experiences" show on television.

On the air, Art's rules were simple: with no bullshit involved, just tell your tale, or you get the boot. Give the people proof or don't bother to call in.

Alan spent endless hours listening to the soothing, seventies-smooth voice of Art.

Listening as he helped his callers find the strength needed to confess their tales of intrigue and fear, Alan developed a fanboy crush on the late-night DJ. Artemis Belliard

And like any fanboy Alan began to dig into Artemis's real life separate from the *Kingdom*, finding it almost as interesting as the midnight tales he helped bring out every night.

Having started out his career in the rebellious rock and roll days of California radio before moving out to the desert in the mid-seventies, Artemis was always evasive about why he would leave a successful career in FM Radio for the desert.

When asked why he would spend all his accumulated wealth to build the isolated radio station, Artemis would only hint, "When given a sign, you gotta make the turn brother..."

Notorious for avoiding personal appearances, Art built an almost cult-life fiefdom of followers that fed off his secretive nature and dubious content.

Despite the unlikely chance for its survival, being a small radio enterprise based in Nowheresville, Nevada; the "*Kingdom*" carved out a place in a world quickly being taken over by color television and FM radio.

For thirty years, in the dark of the night, it was his voice that brought you the "truth" no one wanted to tell you.

Photographs of Artemis were hard to come by, the few pictures of Alan could find on an old radio blog, were grainy and hastily scanned in. With his curly red hair and slim physique, Artemis Belliard looked just like his voice sounded.

Polyester butterfly shirt, neatly trimmed beard, and dark rimmed glasses; Art could have been that groovy, art teacher that was always your favorite because he seemed real.

This was the vision of a man you wanted to trust.

Coming home from the game store at Parkdale Mall to find his Mom was off in Port Arthur to get her scotch-induced two-step boogie on, Alan celebrated.

Like most teenagers, he was happy to be free of parental influence; even if his mom were the best mom in the world. There was always something electric about being left alone on a weekend night, whether you did anything exciting or not.

Taking time to “shake the snake,” Alan snagged a couple of cold ones from the fridge, checked the front and back doors one last time before heading back into his man-cave of mystery and the waiting tales of the *Kingdom*.

Quickly clinking on the bookmark, Alan opened up the "archives," start the next streaming audio clip in line while cracking the top on his tasty taurine laced drink.

There was no title on the track, the only identifier was the date: September 21, 1986. It could have been a meta-data problem but the file loaded easily, so Alan paid it no mind.

As the audio came up, Alan noticed immediately that whoever had edited the podcast for streaming had cut it awkwardly, leaving in a large chunk of commercial.

Ordinarily the recordings were not made from the masters, merely copies of rebroadcasts, so occasionally a clip would make it in along with a familiar reel to reel hiss.

But this time almost the entire commercial break was there. and the clarity of the broadcast was crystal clear.

As a jingle for the cup of coffee that was "good to the last drop" finished, the program was started an hour into a broadcast and Art, with his caramel smooth voice was reminding his listeners to call in on the talk lines.

"If calling from the East Coast the number is 347-555-2368. If you are calling from the Nation of Nevada or west of the Rocky Mountains, dial 775-555-4100. And of course the Wild Card line for those that absolutely gotta be heard right now is 800-555-9355.

The *Kingdom* had been off the air for over a decade and yet Alan almost fell out of his chair scrambling for a pen. Scribbling the phone numbers down on a piece of scraggly notebook paper.

Leaned back precariously in his captain's chair to staring up at the little piece of paper as Art brought the conversation back on track.

"Coming back from our break, for those listeners just tuning in, we have a caller who claims to be approaching Groom Lake via air in a private aircraft. Tyler?

"Are you still there Tyler? I think you are making a serious mistake and you need to reconsider this rash action before it's too late..."

For some reason he felt energized, like he had found the code to decipher the Beale codex the secrets behind the Oak Island treasure pit.

There is no real reason to celebrate these numbers, he thought. It was more than likely they had long since been assigned to a new address or company and yet as he stared at them till they began to swim in his watery vision.

Alan's gut told him there was something important about writing those numbers down but before he could figure it out his attention was drawn back by a terrified, panic cry and gunfire on the *Kingdom* broadcast.

The rogue pilot attempting to buzz Groom Lake found the government played no games when it came to protecting national security. Audio insanity crashed through his speaker followed by an errie empty dial tone.

The aviator hadn't quite found the answers he wanted but had received an answer all the same forcing Artemis to dump into an impromptu commercial break.

It made Alan wonder if it could have possibly been real.

Rewinding the crash sequence over and over again until the website froze, Alan listened for anything that might give it away as canned sound or board effects.

After an hour of playing with it in pro tools, clearing away all tracks but the crash it all seemed clean on manipulation. In the end he had to admit to himself that he had no idea.

Reloading the *Kingdom* website feed cold, Alan felt goose-pimples spread out on his arms as he realized the commercials and call in numbers were gone. the recording starting directly at the intro.

"Coming back from our break, for those listeners just tuning in, we have back to a caller who claims to be approaching Groom Lake via air in a private aircraft. Tyler?

"Are you still there Tyler?"

The call-in numbers were gone from the recording and yet sitting there on his desk written in his messy handwriting there they were. Nothing in the world short of that file being removed or replaced in the last hour could have explain how an audio file could change like that.

Starting over several times, Alan listened to the recording over and over, only to find that same cut.

Alan might have continued doing it all night, tying to convince himself he wasn't crazy if the site didn't lock up again; refusing to be shut down or restarted again. Frustrated and confuse he picked up the paper and stared at it quizzically.

If he had imagined it all and was going crazy, then those numbers laying in front of him should be crap, pure figments of his sub-conscious mind.

Should I call? Alan asked himself, his curiosity peaked.

There was nothing in the world that would satiate his need to prove their validity beyond calling.

Yeah, he would probably end up in a very short, one sided conversation with some Chinese take-out joint in Vegas but it really was the only way to get it out of his head.

Lex Parsimoniae, or Occam's razor: other things being equal, a simpler explanation is better than a more complex one.

Picking up his iPhone, Alan dialed the Wildcard line without a moment of hesitation and the number began to ring through...

*

"You are live on the Wild Card line! What's on your mind caller?"

Like a fan-boy close enough to smell the perfume of his favorite starlet, Alan completely fucking lost it. The phone slipped free of his hand and bounced harmlessly on the shag carpet as he almost flipped over backward in the chair trying to catch it.

Wrapping his fingers around the textured case, Alan brought the phone back up to his ear, just in time to hear, "Are you still there caller?"

"Uh.... Yeah, sorry about that, Art."

"Not a problem, caller. So who are you and what's on your mind this fine evening in the Kingdom of the Night?"

"Ummm... I'm Alan, first time caller, hardcore, long time listener from Texas, sir," Alan paused for a second and then just blurted it out: "To be honest, I'm kinda surprised to be talking with you."

“Well thanks for the compliment there, Alan from Texas. I know it’s hard to get through on the lines sometimes, but it is always a pleasure to greet a new voice to the airwaves here in the kingdom. Broadcast from sea to shining sea, thousands of folks right on the edge of their seats waiting to hear what mysteries from deep in the heart of Texas you have bring to the table.

“So, what tales of intrigue and interest do you have for our listeners tonight, Alan from Texas?”

“Okay Art, can you answer a question for me?” It was definitely Artemis Belliard on the phone, that was certain but a voice could be manipulated. “What's the date?”

“Oh no, have we got a visitor from the future on the line tonight! Have you come to warn us of the terrors that await, like our good friend, John Titor? Or are you from the past? Terrified and lost in a world not your own?”

Alan imagined the man smiling behind the mic, stroking his beard or cleaning his glasses as he dealt so calmly with another time-traveler.

"To answer your question Alan, in the Kingdom of the Night it is September 21st, 1986 for another two hours."

Alan put the iPhone on speaker and brought the *Kingdom* website back up on his monitor. The streaming feed was still there but it wasn't playing anymore, stuck in what seemed to be perpetual buffering mode, both freezing the program and keeping it from closing. But it still clearly displayed the date: ***September 21, 1986***.

"Still there, Alan?"

"Yeah, just trying to work out the math in my head,"

Math my ass, Alan thought. Trying to give his brain a chance to figure out what to say was more like it.

"I guess you could say I'm in the future."

"And what year are you from?"

"Well, where I'm at its 2012."

"So you not actually in our time frame, Alan? Wherever you are, it's still 2012 not 1986?"

"Exactly, Art. The clock on my computer reads 11:02 p.m. on September 21, 2012."

"What could possibly be so important twenty-two years from now, that you feel the need to shatter the theory of a linear time matrix?"

Alan didn't know what to say, leaving a big blank 30 second hole in the broadcast.

"Quite right, Alan. Take a moment, collect your thoughts. All the secrets of the future and more after this short commercial break..."

And for just a second, the line went mute before Artemis jumped on the line.

“Look, kid,” his voice not quite the gentle genial host anymore; rough, and edgy like a man who didn't have the patience for games. “I don't have time for a long drawn out story that ends in indigestible B.S. Either you got something to say or you don't, and I'm not going to give you more than three minutes of live airtime to waste.

“People listen to the show because I put a great big spotlight on the real crazy in the universe and the world laps it up like Pavlovian dogs when I ring my bell. You are not ringing my bell, brother....Do we understand each other?”

Alan had played enough RPGs to know when he was being railroaded, and when being railroaded, the best answer was bring some aggro in return.

“On September 11, 2001, four planes will be hi-jacked by Middle Eastern extremists in Boston, Norfolk, and Newark....

“Two of these planes will be flown into the World Trade Center Towers, one will crash into the Pentagon, and the last will crash into a farmer's field in Pennsylvania.

“These acts of terrorism basically start a global war on terror that lasts for over a decade, causing American's to sacrifice their civil liberties in the name of security.

“How's that for ringing the bell, Artemis?”

“Right on, my time-traveling friend, right on,” That righteous, on-air, big daddy voice was firmly back in place as Art relaxed, knowing which direction to drive the conversation in. “I dig where you are going with this. But let's not start out with gloom and doom right out of the gate.

“Give me some positive stuff and then we sell that front sell the tragedy to blow their brains out towards the end of the show. Here we go, kid.

“Coming out of the break in five seconds...four seconds...three seconds....”

Alan could hear the last of the call numbers go out just as Art stepped up to the mike.

“Crashing through the ten o'clock hour here in the *Kingdom of Night*, we are fortunate to have a special visitor with us tonight.

“A young man who just confessed to me during the break that he has come bearing dire warnings about the future.

“So Alan the future man.... What's the skinny, brother? What's your story?

“Are you part of a secret military project that escaped at great peril from your handlers?

“Are you a member of a special cabal of scientists from the future sent back to help fix the ills of the world?”

Taking a deep breath, Alan just let his voice lead him...

"Art, I'm just a kid. I'm seventeen years old, live in an ordinary house, in an ordinary neighborhood with my mom in a little backwater town deep in the heart of Southeast Texas. I have never been a part of any government project, as far as I know.

"I just heard your call out for callers on my computer, dialed the number, and somehow I'm having a conversation with somebody that hasn't been on the air for almost a decade. It's almost like I'm chatting with a ghost in the machine... weird, right?"

Playing with his iPhone on the desk, spinning it nervously, Alan suddenly just started to talk.

"Like, I'm on an cellular phone, which probably didn't exist in your time. It doesn't require any cords, except to charge, and broadcasting not just phone call but computer signals through the air like radio.

But what's really special about it, inside this "phone" is more computing power than was used to put men on the moon."

Over the next hour Alan discussed the world's recent past with Art and his guests, cluing them in on little parts of the future he didn't think would hurt anything.

Answers that were supposed to just fill in the blanks, like iPhones and Wi/Fi end up eating large blocks of air time as Alan found himself having to explain concepts that were basic conveniences of life to him but still science fiction in 1986.

From the growth of and dominance of personal computers and the birth of the Internet to hybrid cars, Alan tried his best to explain the ordinary and extraordinary.

When they went to the mandatory station ID at the top of the hour, Art announced, “Man, this could be the best broadcast of my career, kid,” the excitement in his voice pure electric.

“You just keep it coming, kid.

“The phone lines are jammed packed and going nuts, so I'm gonna mix in more callers when we come out of break.

"Everybody wants to talk to you and we haven't even given them the steak yet!"

When the lines opened in the second hour Alan continued to play trivia master with the help of his computer and Google as a steady line of of random callers peppered him with question about the near future.

Do the Russians win the cold war? *No.*

Does a nuclear war occur in your time line? *No.*

Have the aliens landed yet? *Could be.*

Who killed Kennedy? *Really..? I'm just a kid with a computer, not God.*

Do the Saints ever win a Super Bowl? *Yes, but all the poor people that love them live in Houston.*

Alan did his best to keep up with their questions, explaining what he knew and embellishing the rest with the help of Google, Wikipedia and the web.

It actually made him feel bad that he hadn't paid more attention in Miss Boudreaux's world civics class, but who plans for the moment in time when you can change the past with a history lesson?

A question occurred to Alan, as his conversation with the good people of 1986 lingered into the dark night. What if the things he was revealed were having some form of deleterious effect on the universe?

If things were going to change, wouldn't it have already happened?

Shouldn't new memories be flooding his mind as people changed the world with his forbidden knowledge?

Shouldn't the effect of knowledge from the future injected into the past have an instantaneous affect on his present?

Turning slowly around his room, everything looked exactly the way it was before he started the phone call. He had to admit his head was a little fuzzy but Alan tossed it up to having been up too late mixed with the excitement of his unexpected auditory adventure.

Artemis was almost overwhelmed with excitement, Alan could almost visualize him rushing around his tiny desert studio trying to keep up with it all.

“Coming out of this break, we hit'em in the mouth with the dire and dread, Alan. I mean scare them to their core with your story of death and destruction in the skies over New York.

“But just to warn you, after about ten minutes, I'm gonna bring on a friend to help finish up the conversation. Do you know Major Frank Dames, or heard him on my show before?”

Alan had heard of him alright.

This was the guy who claimed to have taught soldiers to kill with their minds, had infiltrated Area 51, and supposedly cracked the Montague Project wide open.

Having heard him on the show multiple times and Alan firmly believed the man to be a pretentious douche.

"He is a total dick, Artemis! Do you have to bring him on?" Alan actually whined about it like he was a little kid.

The guy really was an asshole.

"Alan, I wouldn't ask -- you have done the show a great service tonight -- but he called in personally during the last hour and after I told him your story about the planes, he really wants to talk with you.

"I have never heard such interest in his voice before, and I know he can be a little stand-offish but as long as you don't cuss him out on air, I am fine with you defending yourself.

"Remember F-bombs on the radio costs lots of money here in the past just like they do where you come from okay?"

"Roger that, Art, no F-bombs."

"Groovy kid, groooovy!" Artemis cleared his throat before lighting up his mike.

"And thanks to *Purina Dog Chow* for bringing us through another hour of reaching into the murky night sky of the unexplained and impossible here in the Doctor's office.

"From sea to shining sea we are the beacon, America. Calling out on the radio waves for tales of the strange and wondrous world around us and tonight has been no exception, ladies and gentlemen.

"For some inexplicable reason... Be it solar flares bending "cellular" signals through space and time or a portal of fate due to the Meso-American prophecy of 2012, tonight we have been blessed by a fortuitous connection tonight.

"A view into a bright glorious future? Are these echoes from another another plane of existence? A string vibrating out of tune with the great mystery that is the universe?

"Tonight, we have had the privilege of a brief glimpse into a future that could be our present in a blink of an eye. All brought to us by the voice of a child that will not be born for another decade.

"Young Alan from Southeast Texas, circa 2012, has answered all your questions, and with the morning nigh here in the Kingdom of the Night, Alan has saved his most dire of warning for all of us as his final message.

"So young time traveler, what great tragedy awaits us Americans in the near future?"

"Art....On September 11th," was all Alan was able to get out before the screen on his iPhone just went black.

**

With the lengthy conversation on speaker phone, Alan had completely managed to forget about charging his phone.

Knowing the bitch was a notorious power hog he couldn't quite understand how he completely miss the low battery notice. Not that any of that meant anything now, there was no doubt it was dead.

Panic set in quickly as he plugged it into his computer, waiting anxiously for the battery symbol and open apple to signal a restart. Staring at the tiny screen, the consequences of his actions began to to take hold.

Had he just blown his one chance at stopping the worst event in modern American history by bullshitting about personal computers and alien invasions?

Looking it up on the internet it was all still there. Those terrifying pictures; Tower 2, the falling man, the canyons of dust. 9/11 was forever cemented in history and no boy from southeast Texas was going to stop that.

It was a tragedy but it made total sense. He hadn't talked about it on air, which meant it was going to happen no matter what. Right?

Just then at his lowest point, Alan's phone lit up and he slid his index finger across the slick touch screen to unlock it before scrambling to hit redial.

"**Beep... Beep... Beep... This number has been disconnected or is no longer in service. Please check the number and try again.**
Beep...Beep...Beep."

"What was the point in that?" Alan screamed out to no one.

His teenage rage welling up and exploding in an exhausted *"FUUUCCCKK!"* before slamming his head down on the desk in frustration.

In that same way a junkie goes back to an empty pipe just one last time, Alan tried the other two numbers only to be greeted by the same recorded answer.

And as quickly as it had begun, Alan's foray into the dark world of the *Kingdom* was suddenly over.

Shutting down the miscellaneous windows on his desktop, Alan logged back onto *The Kingdom* website to look up the mystery audio file that had started out the night's adventures.

It was now clearly marked with the title: **September 21, 1986: "Open Calls - Shot Down Over Area 51, Alan: The Time-Traveling Teen, & Major Frank Dames"**

*So it was real....*Alan thought to himself.

Hand shaking above the mouse, he was almost nervous to hear the sound of his own voice but was about to right click on the file to start it anyways.

It was that exact moment his bladder let him know that the adrenaline and caffeine in his body wasn't strong enough to keep the urge to piss painless any longer.

Jumping up from his comfy black chair, Alan headed down the hallway to the bathroom, passing the big western bar clock on the wall that read ten after one. The house was still quiet, so Alan assumed his Mom was still enjoying her Saturday night in Port Arthur.

He was glad she wasn't here, what would he tell her?

Hi mom! Guess what I did to night? I almost changed history but forgot to charge my phone....

What would he tell anyone that would make them believe any of it?

Standing above the toilet in the dark, the rush of urine leaving his body was such a relief that Alan almost fell backwards stretching his back and neck.

Staring up at the at the cracked paint on the ceiling, it was only then Alan noticed the movement of the trees outside flickering on the drywall above his head.

Their shadows were blowing about crazily on the humidity stained plaster, just like they do before a coming storm. The news hadn't mentioned anything about a storm-front moving in off the Gulf overnight but that didn't mean there wasn't a late night mover heading in off the water.

Alan wandered into the living room, hoping to catch a good look at the approaching tempest from the large bay window in the living room; there is nothing like a late night storm. The trees whipped about as a strange wind buffered the house but not a single drop of rain fell on the window pane.

Standing there, staring out into the dark Alan was blinded by shattering glass as the front window imploded on him, tossing him several feet from the broken bay window.

Laying in the wreckage; stunned while his mind vibrating from the explosion, Alan barely noticed the smoke charge arced into the room and exploding on the couch starting a fire.

Alan choked on the acrid smoke but couldn't make himself move as the sounds of booted feet followed the crash of the front door being kicked off its hinges.

A sharp knee landed on his spine as someone silently grabbed his arms and cuffed him, the sharp edge of plastic zip ties biting at his soft wrists.

It wasn't until the rough fabric of a black canvas hood being shoved over his head did Alan start to recover from his concussion-induced fugue and then the panic began to set in. Pulled up by his armpits, Alan was dragged out of the house fighting and screaming to no avail.

He was no threat to whoever had locked him down, their strong hands holding him in place, no matter how hard he fought. The warm night air caressed his bruised skin as the sound of ringing began to subside in his ears.

As the wind started to buffer at the bag enclosing his head, Alan could have sworn he heard the soft whup of helicopter blades before being thrown down into a hard metal seat and handcuffed down.

Despite having never ridden in one didn't stop Alan from identifying the vibration associated with a helicopter as it rumbled through his ass and up his bruised spine.

Although far quieter than any helicopter he had ever seen or heard, Alan's suspicions were quickly confirmed as his stomach lurched as the pilot lifted off quickly.

With the hood still firmly placed on his head, Alan had no idea who these people were or where they were going. The only clue was that he wasn't alone was the warm leg of someone else sitting next to him as it briefly rubbed up against him while the flew off into the night.

Someone gently place a pair of old style big can headphones on his head over the hood, that fully cut off any outside sound. It was suddenly very dark, deathly quiet, and even though he didn't believe it were possible, Alan discovered an even higher level of fear just before a familiar voice creeped in to his ears.

“Hey Kid. Let me introduce myself, I'm Colonel Frank Dames. Unfortunately we didn't get a chance to chat before and I really wanted to have a conversation with you. So stay calm and don't panic, you are not in any immediate danger.

“You know... it wasn't so hard to find you. It was all about the timing.

"Your comment about 9/11 set off massive alarms in high places, son. My remote viewers had been seeing those same images for years before your impromptu visit to the *Kingdom* radio show. Despite the small differences, what you said was close enough to what we already knew for me to take an interest in your life.

"Once I figured out which Alan you were it was just a matter of waiting for you to make the phone call. We got some amazing results tonight kid, some really great evidence on how wormholes work and how small they can be. Once your system finished downloading that file, we knew you had broken the connection and it was safe to move in.

"Believe me, kid. It never pays to mess with unstable wormholes."

Alan tried to yell out that he had no idea how any of this had happened, but all that came out of his mouth was a muffled, sobbing mess.

“Calm down, kid. Like I said,there is nothing gonna happen to you or your momma. She's taking a right restful nap now and won't remember a thing after my teams take your house apart down to the foundation looking for any residual evidence of a rift in any form.

“You two are going for a short vacation on the government dime, Alan,” and without warning Colonel Frank Dames’ voice suddenly shifted. His tone deepened, warming up, suddenly very supportive and unmistakable.

“So just relax, Kid.... It's gonna be groovy kid, just groovy!”

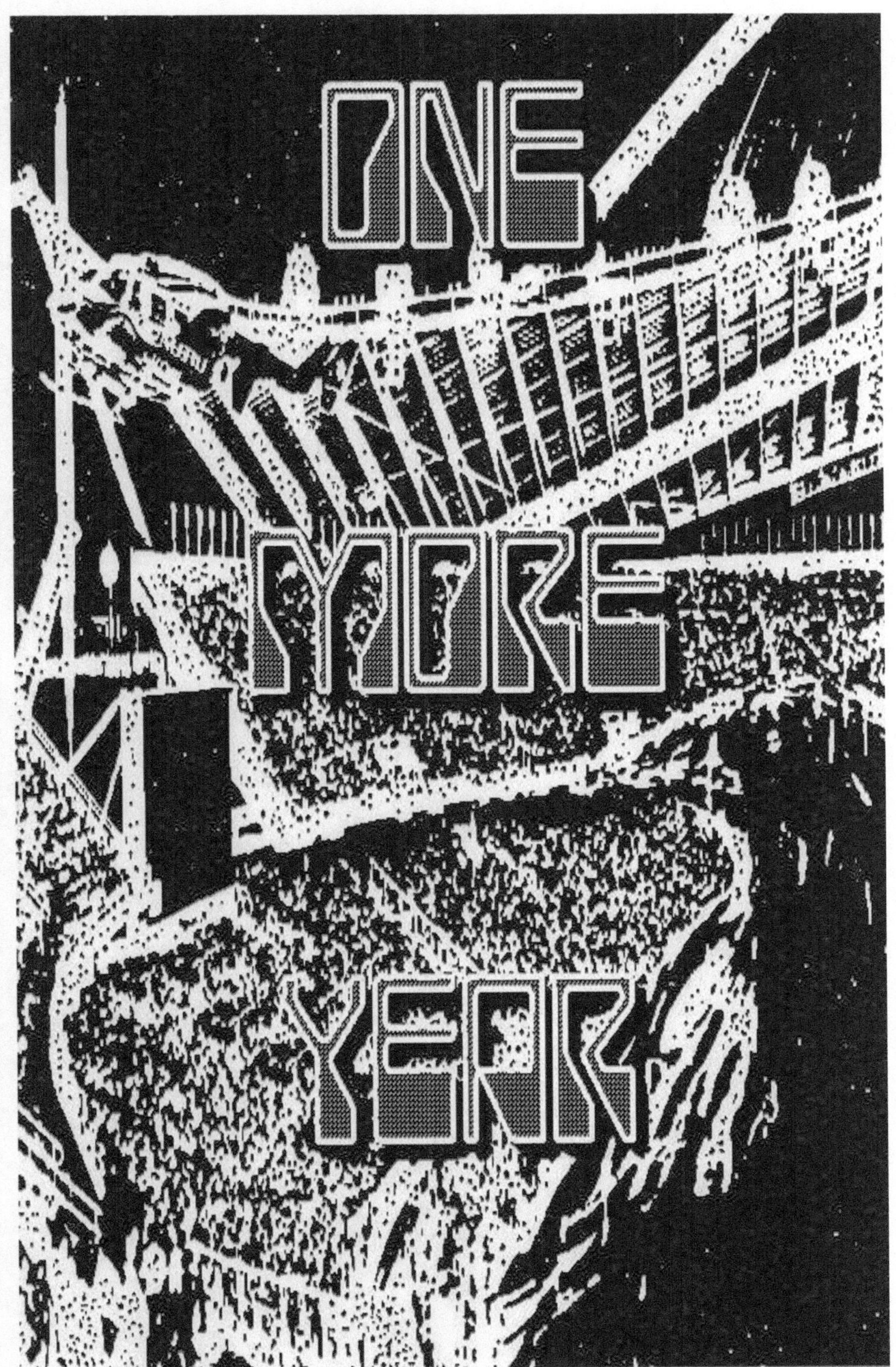
ONE
MORE
YEAR

One More Year

Desperation is an unyielding opponent. It never stops.

Like a locomotive with its throttle snapped off, desperation just keeps pouring on the steam 'til something breaks, and you either survive or die.

It's that simple.

Athletes and warriors have known this fact since the first time two humans looked at each other; racing across an open savanna in search of the last piece of food or to escape a rapidly-approaching predator.

Desperation opens up every sense to its maximum level. Every advantage from a billion years of evolution is right there at your finger tips.

What you do with it is all up to you.

As Jackson "Black Jack" Greene lay motionless, strapped firmly to a hover-gurney while medical personnel buzzed around him; trying desperately to shield him from the steady drizzle of rain pouring down on the field and unblinking eyes of the media.

Please... please....

The word jumbled around in Jackson's brain like some mad painting only he could see.

The letters drifting in and out of nowhere, as the signals from his brain to his lips seem to get lost somewhere along the way.

*

Three minutes, sixteen seconds.

In an ordinary man's life, three minutes and sixteen seconds is barely time to smoke a cigarette, collect your lunch and get out the door before the bus rumbles down the street.

In Jackson Greene's world, three minutes and sixteen seconds is an eternity filled with complex geometry, statistical probability, and Newtonian physics.

All made infinitely more difficult when somebody is trying to kill you at full speed.

With three minutes and sixteen seconds left in the fourth quarter, a monstrous linebacker broke through a weak point in Dallas' offensive line. Punching, ripping, twisting and turning his way past Jackson's stalwart million-credit mountains of protective flesh. Eyes trained on only one target.

There's the door, baby....

The linebacker was on target.

This was the ticket.

That highlight reel moment that would put his team in the championship, guarantee a fat contract to feed his family for the rest of his career.

Froth coated his lips and mouthpiece like a horse chomping furiously on its bit. Every piece of DNA in the linebacker's body was tapped directly into his primal self, overloading the mind with every bit of fight and determination left in his desperately exhausted body.

Locking on to Jackson Greene's wide unprotected back like a missile, he launched himself into sports history.

**

The ironman of professional football, Jackson Greene knew this blitz inside and out. He had seen it ten thousand times over his storied career.

His record-shattering 540 game career and unprecedented six world championships would make him a permanent resident at the Hall of Fame in Canton.

Jackson Greene was a corporate entity built on a lifetime of sacrifice and sweat. A living machine that pumped blood like nitro on the gridiron.

A legend who would always be your number one hero in the great nation of New Texas.

His rugged face was on t-shirts, holo-walls, soda cans, and in the living rooms of football fans every Sunday for over thirty years. During the season the team paid for an entire building in downtown Dallas to stand tall as electric effigy to his magnificence.

Jack's reassuring face lit up in by a billion organic light emitting diodes while he smiled, waved, and occasionally threw a holographic pass down to his fans below.

As seconds ticked off the clock before the rain-slick ball snapped back to his tacky covered fingers. Jack called out a play shift, certain of his decision and the results.

A short throw to the tight end outside should take care of the blitz. An easy five yards and second down.

There was only one problem with his decision.

Life.

Feet once nimble enough to dance on the roof of a limousine after the draft, didn't react quickly enough as his fifties set in.

Eyes that once saw the tiniest hole in the best coverage schemes now played tricks with his depth perception, shadows playing havoc in the bright blue-white halogen lights above the field.

Jackson's perception of how fast the game was really moving was off by a mere three quarters of a second but that was enough.

The raging linebacker leapt from his feet, striking Jackson directly between his shoulder pads and spine protector with his steel reinforced face mask. The impact was like getting struck in the back by a cannonball at close range.

Jackson finally found himself at that place in the universe where everything is statistically probable if you do it long enough.

The strange geometry where the exact angle and manner in which the hardened steel laced, carbon-fiber infused face mask wedged its way through the layers of Jackson's protective gear was an anomaly that could only occur on the longest of time-lines.

This math lesson was a devastating one, the violent impact shattering the vertebrae up and down his back like frozen high tension cables from a failing bridge.

Camera flashes exploded all over the maximum capacity mega-stadium, lighting up the field like the sun for just a moment as the people on three planets watched Jack's head snapped back in Holo-HD.

The ball, once clasped in his iron grip, rolled freely away from his broken body when Jackson rag-dolled across the brilliant blue terra-formed field.

***

"Not one more year! Do you hear me, Jack? Not one MORE!"

Samantha Greene couldn't bear the pain, the fear, the spotlight anymore... Not after 30 years of the same circus.

"I'm fucking fifty-one years old and as hot as a forty-year-old. If you make me leave, I'll be the hottest cougar in town with half your shit, Jack!"

They had told him not come back this year.

Forget the endorsements, forget the money and fame, forget the championships, forget the rings.

"It is too dangerous to play professional football at fifty-two Jack! You could die, asshole!" Samantha screamed at him, tears streaming down her cinnamon skin as she packed her bags.

Jackson had never allowed anyone else to make his decisions for him. The thought of quitting left him cold and naked like a frightened child, couldn't she see that?

He would be nothing without the game. Nothing.

"I don't love you anymore, Jack."

Samantha Greene would abandon their multi-million dollar home outside of Austin on the same day Jack left for training camp in Dallas.

"This is who I am!" Jack screamed at her as she walked out the door.

****

Dark dreams haunted Jack's fitful sleep.

The roar of a crowd in an empty stadium filled his head. The sound echoing back and forth like a massive wave smashing into a concrete tidal wall. The vibrations seemed to tear through him, stealing a little bit of his life with each and every pass.

Even deep in a drug induced coma Jackson dreamed of the crowd's adulation.

But he was all alone. Pain was Jackson Greene's only reward for hubris.

The machine was broken, soon to be forgotten.

*****

Four months.

This was how long Jackson spent in a medically induced coma, recovering from injuries he could never feel.

The surgeons said Jack's spinal cord had split at the T1 thoracic cluster and worked its way down; the delicate tissue shredded from bone fragments of his shattered vertebrae ripped apart by the impact.

Blessed by overall health, they all agreed he was lucky to have survived an injury so devastating.

One hundred, twenty-two days.

Fractures in the skull below the right eye, right shoulder completely rebuilt after the impact with the turf, four broken ribs, a fractured hip, crushed ulna and radius bones in his throwing arm. Add in the surgery required to fuse his vertebrae, as well as multiple intense stem cell therapy sessions to reconnect his spine.

Two thousand, nine hundred, twenty-eight hours.

The doctors in charge reported it was the worst trauma case they had ever dealt with that didn't involve some form of vehicle. Thanks to the nano-mite nerve conductors implanted in his spine Jack could feel his extremities but according to the white coats, regaining total mobility was not realistic. Science and medicine could only restore so much.

Jackson couldn't imagine a life less desirable than being trapped in a chair. His whole life had been built upon physicality. The subtle curves of his arms had once been the star of their own photo layout in Cosmo.

His face had graced the covers of every sports rag in the system. Millions of men and women stalked his movements online from Istanbul to Mars Dome. Jackson Greene was a celestial superstar, an icon for the ages.

Icons do not piss in a bag or need someone's help to wipe their ass!

Jackson was sequestered in his Austin compound, hidden away from prying eyes to heal as the sports entertainment industry soldiered on without him. In collusion with his agent Manny Whilton, the team and League were doing their best to keep the true nature of his health and recovery on the hush-hush.

Unfortunately with trillions of dollars in the mix, the secrecy was more about covering up the truth instead of protecting Jack's legacy.

The League had been lambasted by critics about safety concerns since the early part of the millennium. As the accumulated knowledge of medicine, with the help of corporate cash and scientific momentum, reached a level akin to art, it became obvious how dangerous the world's most exciting game really was.

Rule changes would cost the League millions of viewers and billions in credits and they knew it. This was an issue they couldn't allow to fester.

So the lawyers went into overdrive and like most problems in the world, when you throw enough money at a problem, it will go away.

Player salaries increased exponentially due to "personal responsibility" investment clauses designed specifically to help pay for medical bills. Long detailed contracts full of concessions and bonuses in exchange for the player involved to absolve the League of any responsibility for long-term health implications.

Covered from all angles legally, Jackson Greene's injuries wouldn't cause more of an uproar besides the loss of a living legend to time and age.

And yet to lose Jackson Greene, their most recognizable superstar in such a violent way made the League lawyers and accountants antsy. They could feel the creep of negative attention on the horizon, and wanted nothing to do with that kind of spotlight again.

Millions were spent to keep a lid on the details of Jackson's recovery and with the start of training camp; with his replacement already in the fold, the time for keeping secrets was almost done. With no word coming out of his reps in Dallas to the media, it was just assumed Jack had quietly retired.

As the team prepared to march off to war without him, he stopped being a nightly conversation on the net even in Dallas.

It was a blessing he slept through his body healing itself and becoming socially irrelevant at the same time. His mind and ego probably wouldn't have been able to recover.

******

It would take Jack days to figure out where he was and what had happen after waking from his medically induced coma with a terrible taste in his mouth and eyes that couldn't focus. It didn't take long for the reality of his enfeebled condition to set in.

His body no longer his own and despite being surrounded by a platoon of private doctors and nurses, Jack felt truly alone for the first time in his adult life.

Samantha never came back.

Though his room was filled with neat orderly piles of well wishes and gifts from around the world, none were from him. In Jack's mind it felt as if no one cared about the fate that had befallen him.

Why should they care?

In his own eyes, Jack had become a pathetic creature, trapped within a shattered body and it had darkened his heart, filling him with rage.

Like any wounded animal, the medical staff kept him as comfortable as could be expected but kept their distance. First class care was arranged by the team, but paid for out of his own wallet and absolutely no expense was spared.

Every light, television, phone, thermostat and computer in the house was voice programmed to give him some control over his environment.

None of it did anything to lighten his mood. His condition was taking a dark toll on his very soul.

"New Email Jack." the feminine voice of his computer announced. Her tones lilting and soft, designed specifically to help alleviate some of Jack's darker moments.

"Open" he croaked out from between parched lips.

"To: Jackson Greene

From: Unknown Address"

"Dear Mister Greene,

"Life is not always about what was lost.

"Instead, consider what can be gained from losing.

"Your pain is unceasing, your mind stretched to its limit, and death has becomes your only respite.

"Action is required by those of us with the means to do so."

"Your Friend,

Gregor Litwinczuk M.D., PhD."

The message left Jackson drawing a complete blank. Hundreds of doctors had been through these halls since the accident, not one of which he could remember their name and he would have recognized that name.

"Identity search, Gregor Litwinczuk M.D." Jack called out to his computer which silently brought up a search engine and began compiling likely candidates in the screen mounted above Jack's bed. The only result was a thirty-five-year-old article authored by a polish professor Leopold Stronoski on the study of genetics from Sweden.

In a world where everyone had some form of presence on the net, Gregor Litwinczuk's lack of a digital identity was strange to say the least.

"Email, Manny."

Jack sent off a quick message to his agent, instructing Manny to find out exactly who this mysterious doctor was and to keep him as far from the compound as he could if anything seemed shady.

The last thing he needed was another vulture in his life.

****

It was late in the evening, the sun long having passed into the western sky, when Jack awoke from a fitful nightmare, reaching out for someone who wasn't there.

Lifting a couple of inches above his sheet before collapsing under his own weight, Jack swore out at the darkness; cursing the world for his own weakness. The lack of response from his body was a frustrating gift that never stopped giving.

Bringing some relief from his irritation, a cool wash cloth brushed over his wrinkled brow causing Jack to turn his head.

Expecting one of the familiar nurses, Jackson turned to thank them only to be taken aback by the cracked, wizened face of an elderly man smiling down at him from his bedside.

“Hope I didn’t frighten you, young man. With age comes a bit of stealth that is quite unexpected and most don’t understand,” the ancient figure ground out in a heavily accented voice.

Grasping Jackson's docile hand between his dry palms, he shook it gently before laying it back down by his side, “Doctor Gregor Leopold Litwinczuk at your service, Mister Greene.”

“How the hell did you get in my house?!”

“I was authorized at the door, of course. A Manny Whilton sent word ahead that I had permission to examine you.”

Dropping the wet washrag into a bowl on the night-stand, the shambling old man pulled the chair closer to the bed and sat down as Jackson glanced up at the clock on his monitor.

"At one a.m.?"

"Time is a commodity dealt by young, ambitious, or greedy men, Mister Greene. Once you get to our age time lacks validity, no? The regimented ticking of when we can or can't do things suddenly seems irrelevant when face to face with one's mortality.

"I say if there is business to be done, then do it, no matter what the civility of the clock says."

"Okay... So, what miracle cure have you come to sell me, Doc?" There was no disguising the derision in Jack's voice. He had grown weary of the poking and prodding of faceless doctors.

"Oh no, Mister Greene, you misunderstand." A wide yellow toothed grin spread out from beneath the Doctor's scraggly salt & pepper mustache. "There are no retainers, insurance cards, co-pays or deductibles. I am here to give you a one-time gift.

"I'm here to give you your life back."

Jack laughed nervously while wondering how quickly security and staff would react if he shouted out for help.

"Ah, yes! Good! Laughter is good Mister Greene. I want you to laugh for many years." The doctor stood to quickly remove his jacket, which he hung on the back of the chair before returning to his seat at Jack's bedside.

"Do you know of Telomeric Gene Therapy?"

"Hell, no. The only thing I know about medicine is to take what you guys tell me."

"Then we shall move forward simply. Confusion about what we are about to do is unacceptable for the leap of faith you have to undertake."

Taking a second to organize his thoughts, the Doctor stroked his moustache before continuing. “Surely you know that everything organic on our planet is built upon genes, correct?”

“Yeah, they look like curved ladders, right?” Jack almost felt insulted; he did go to college, even if it had been over thirty years ago.

“Precisely!” The doctor’s face lit up, his hands gesturing every phrase as if he were lecturing students instead of one involuntary audience member.

“As we age, our body creates billions of cells over and over again. We are a cellular factory, built to replace ones destroyed through the basic wear and tear of living, you see? Every time a cell reproduces itself a portion of its DNA splits off, forming another strand of chromosomes.

"At the end of these chromosomes are stretches of DNA called telomeres, and their job is to keep our chromosomes from fraying like worn thread or sticking to each other like tangled wires."

Taking an antique stethoscope from his large black satchel, Litwinczuk casually listened to Jack's heart as he continued his explanation.

"When our chromosomes split at the tips or become tangled together, we start to die. It's that simple.

"Maybe years, maybe months, time does not matter to DNA. Time is irrelevant because what we perceive as aging is in reality just tangled webs waiting for nimble fingers to make order of the chaos."

Jack was starting to lose his patience with this snake oil peddler and the sound of his frustration came out in his voice, "Doc, I've already been through the best nanomite enriched stem cell therapy money can buy, and all they promised was limited mobility."

Staring up at the ceiling, Jack could feel the anger build as he actually said it out loud. “I never thought I would end my days in a chair or with a walker, but they say I don’t have much of a choice anymore.”

“No! Mister Greene, you misunderstand.” The doc's eyes lit up like wildfire, as if the passion behind what he was trying to explain couldn't come out of his mouth fast enough and was being communicated through his excited eyes.

“Stem cells will grow to replace lost cellular mass by cloning the surrounding cells. With Telomeric gene therapy, I propose we turn your whole body into stem cells.”

Reaching down, the Doctor pulled a beaten leather satchel into his lap and rummaged around, “You see, as we age telomeres in our genes die or become dormant. This allows for the inevitable microscopic break down in our bodies.

"In this way, nature controls our species as she does everything else." Crooking his head, the doctor stopped for a moment as a small smile crept on to his raggedy old lips.

"There is an automatic cut off switch for everyone, the end of our lives predestined by something designed into our very building blocks."

"It's actually an ingenious method of population control if you think about it. And using my method of Telomeric Gene Therapy, we can turn on every dormant telomere in your body, producing fresh new cells.

"Your body will heal. Your life will return."

Jackson sat in stunned silence. The madness coming out of this small, squirrel-like man was almost infectious.

For a tiny moment, he actually bought into the insanity, "If what you say is true, how come nobody offered this miracle juice to me before?

"Believe me, in my business there isn't a legal or illegal drug on the planet I haven't tried to hold back the tide."

This was no minor boast as Jack's medicine cabinets looked like a colorful abstract painting long before the latest injury. Uppers, downers, pain killers, erectile dysfunction, heartburn, cream to keep his hair full and lustrous.

All the best meds money could buy and always free from the endless caches of the team doctors.

"Ah, the great machine of western medicine....Do you really put your future in the hands of men so blindly worried about nothing but their own pockets?"

The Doctor's distaste for his western counterparts became obvious by the scowl on his craggy face, "Has anything you were ever given; medicines that were promised to heal you, ever done so without having to take them for the rest of your life?"

The doctor paused for a moment before barreling on. "No need to answer. I see the answers on your face, Mister Greene."

And the truth was Jackson did feel skeptical about his future health after the years of endless shots and "supplements" that kept him together and on the field far longer than nature intended.

Now that they didn't need him anymore, what would become of him? Would the billions he had earned just flow away in an endless river in order to pay for years of suppressing the symptoms and delaying the inevitable.

"Do not allow my distaste for Western medicine fool you, Mister Greene. Telomeric therapy is as a volatile drug regimen as chemotherapy."

From a satchel in his lap, the Doctor pulled free a small patent leather case before placing it delicately back on the floor. "It will unlock mysteries of the world to you that you might never understand, and it most definitely comes with a warning."

Opening it up wide for Jack to see, inside lay three glimmering blue vials and an antique brass syringe, each glinting with their own inner light.

“In this case there are three vials. In your pursuit for true healing never use more than two. It is imperative you understand this! Remember that too much of anything can be a detriment. ”

Again with those eyes, boring deep into Jackson's mind with that gaze, driving home his warning with the most sincere look of madness.

“Abuse it and life will be short as well as painful for you. Life ravages those that tempt fate by thinking of immortality.”

Removing the syringe and a single vial, the doctor barely filled it the glistening blue fluid. Taking hold of the injection port on Jack’s I.V., Litwinczuk popped the needle in and pressed hard on the plunger.

“If used with discretion, all of life will roll out in front of you, the horizon glimmering far in the distance.”

Cleaning the needle with an alcohol towelette, the Doctor placed the syringe back in the box before laying the shiny leather-bound package in Jackson's nightstand.

"You may feel flu-like for one week after each treatment, but effects vary based on the subject."

That wide yellowed smile, appeared again, "Believe me, the outcome of your treatments will make any such discomfort a worthwhile sacrifice."

Deep inside Jack's body, it felt as if someone had tripped a switch; a licking warmth penetrated the flesh, melting through the pain, seeping down deep into the marrow of his bones.

Sleep poured into his mind like an electric blue river, drowning out his consciousness in a splash of shimmering sapphire haze.

Taking a moment to check Jack's vitals, Doctor Gregor Litwinczuk stared down at Jackson Greene's bruised, battered, and beaten body, attached to bevy of blinking, murmuring machines.

This broken man had no idea of the wild ride that was to come, he just hoped Jackson would be strong enough to make the right choices this second time around.

As he packed up his satchel, a small smile crept over the Doctor's withered face before he left as stealthily as he had come in.

****

In the midst of an extraordinary moment, it is the ordinary that fuels the engine of any great storm.

Generally the week of a world championship is organized chaos for any of the mega-cities. With this being London's first championship in almost two decades, the League dumped billions of credits onto the streets of "Ol' Smoke."

The grand old crown of the United Kingdom had quite literally become the greatest show on earth. Eyes across the entire system tuned every night for updates on championship week.

Holo-banners emblazoned with images of hung from every lamp post; the swarthy King George, Union Jack waving gently behind his smiling, affably face, welcomed sports fans to his isle.

Thousands of reporters and millions of fans flew into Heathrow Interstellar from across the solar system, creating a party in London more akin to old New Orleans at the height of Mardi Gras than the opulent jewel of the Euro economic zone.

Three levels above the locker rooms at New Wembley stadium, more than a half a million people shook the earth with the stomping of their feet and created fog in the cold wet sky from the air in their lungs.

Thirty minutes of gladiatorial combat had driven the into a frenzy, each and everyone waiting for that killing blow that would put the game out of reach.

But the real action lie below ground in the carpeted halls and concrete tunnels.

As the revelers above shouted to the heavens, the machinations of a five star resort, broadcasting hub, medical center, police station, and sporting event soldiered on down below.

The inside of the locker rooms were plush, personalized for each team and decked out in all the comforts athletes of their stature had come to expect at this level in the game.

Double stim-stims for those lacking in stamina, G27 series electrolyte drinks stacked high in each locker personalized for the player assigned. Everything these thoroughbred human would need to recover for the second half.

All along the walls, massive holo-screens pumped the live universal feed into every nook and cranny of the stadium.

The talking heads, with high definition smiles and endless inane opinions launched into their spiel. It was time to fill the downtime for the billions out there waiting for the second half by adding their take on the what had unfolded in the first thirty minutes.

"What an unbelievable first half, Davison!!! Four billion people sytem wide have witnessed what could only be described as the single greatest feat in the history of professional sports.

"After what could only be described as dire, possibly career ending injuries in last years playoffs; "Black" Jack Greene and his Dallas machine have roared into Old England like the mythical Lion on a mission.

"So much in the balance... On one side a quest to seal the deal on that that magical seventh world championship ring for Greene.

"On the other, the dream of an undefeated season for the first time since 1972 hangs in the balance for the misfit Moscow Mammoths---"

Slowly the volume on the monitors were lowered as one of the porters under instruction muted the audio and yet there was no silence to be found.

An earthquake-like rumble exploded down the ramp from the field as the entire Dallas team; wet ,bloody and exhausted, barreled down like a freight train.

The once calm locker room explode with activity; the annoying voice of the reporters as well as the sounds of the support staff, was instantly swallowed up by the oddly calming sound of a bustling football team preparing for the second half.

The rip of medical tape stretching out and slapping of shoulder pads. Sharpened cleats clicking on tile accompanied by a chorus of groans from those whose muscles got re-hydrated and worked out before the second half.

All of it blended together into white noise as Jackson Greene leaned back in his locker trying to catch his breath.

Inside he wasn't thinking about winning the game.

Or the pain from his battered body.

Behind his dark visor Jack wasn't thinking anything at all.

Inside, Jackson Green was the calm eye of the hurricane.

****

Being paralyzed does not stop one from thinking he can do the things he always has.

If anything, it reinforces his commitment to do those things again, even if not physically possible.

Every morning since waking from his coma, Jack would momentarily forget his body was wrecked beyond repair. Then he would try to slide from his bed to take a much needed piss.

Normally, that was when he would be rewarded with a couple of inches in movement and an entire days worth of frustration.

This morning would be different.

The chill of cool marble under his feet woke Jackson just enough to make him look down at his legs that hung over the edge of the bed. This in turn caused a look of confusion on his face normally reserved for someone who accidentally does something right.

It only took moments for the realization of what he had just done to take hold in his mind. This was followed quickly by the shadowy memory of his late night visit with the doctor.

Instantaneously the reality of what they had done snapped into place like an old camera coming into focus.

Bending and flexing his body in ways not possible twelve hours earlier, Jackson moved slowly at first, not really sure how far his body would actually go. Once certain his legs wouldn't buckle beneath him like a newborn colt, Jack removed the monitor leads and I.V.'s and head towards the bathroom.

After thirty years in the league, it was no challenge to disengage from the machines and tubes... It was taking out the catheter that actually hurt.

The pain didn't matter to Jack, he was just thankful for feeling something after being numb for so long.

His sudden disconnection from the monitoring system, on the other hand, caused an almost laughable amount of panic amongst the medical staff.

Rushing into his bedroom, the crash team was surprised to find themselves staring at Jack sculpted ass as he took a glorious golden piss of the gods.

Over the next forty-eight hours, Jackson was put through a battery of every exam the med staff could dream up. In the end, only he would know the answers to his miracle recovery.

The shiny black case of Litwinczuk's mysterious blue vials were secreted away from the prying eyes of doctors, lawyers and agents, hidden deep in the drawers of his teak nightstand.

Jack decided early on that the only proof of Doctor Litwinczuk's late night visit would stay his secret. Manny never asked and in the end it was nobody's business why he had recovered. Why should he care about giving anyone an answer?

It didn't take long for word to leak out of Casa Greene. Within days of his "miracle" recovery, rumors mounted on the net. Within hours of the story breaking, Jack released all the medical staff and locked down his Austin compound.

It wasn't as if he was refusing to face the world. He just didn't have time for it.

Jackson Greene had to get back to work. Using the Blue like a supplement, the machine inside him resurfaced. The drive to have purpose again took over as he would sometimes spend eight to ten hours a day in the gym.

It didn't take long for Jack to take note of the serious changes in his body.

As early as two weeks along, scars from four decades of playing the sport faded away to fresh, healthy skin. Gray hairs that once seeped into his chestnut mane were gone, replaced by the thick dark growth of his youth.

Even the calloused, sandpaper-like hands that had gripped a hundred thousand snaps gained a fullness and glow that Jackson had not seen since his thirties. Almost all traces of the sacrifices Jack had made in a lifetime of vainglorious combat were gone.

And he found he couldn't face himself in the mirror anymore.

In the beginning, getting old is difficult for anyone. It takes time to appreciate the nuances and details that life rewards us with for having survived so long. Jack had gotten used to his own grizzled appearance, and the man who stared back at him from the mirror was twenty years younger.

He was still recognizable but this was definitely not his face anymore.

The Doctor has warned him that the Blue had side effects but it imbued Jack with an almost unpleasant energy level. He had to work off constantly just to feel normal and even that didn't completely take the edge off.

Leading up to training camp Jackson met with no one. Not his handlers, not the team reps, no one. Even his loyal agent Manny Whilton couldn't get a call through, which annoyed the money man to no end.

A week before players were scheduled to report to Dalls for camp, Jack picked up the phone and within minutes he restarted the media machine and his career

Once word hit the street that Jackson Greene was looking to make one final run, all the familiar faces started to pop up buzzing with deals and endorsements.

Unfortunately they were all met with disappointment. The normal channels of communication were abandoned. Jackson Greene had shut down the money machine altogether.

He wasn't coming back for the money.

The Dallas organization was naturally suspicious of Jackson's recovery; having been in the small circle of trust during the worst of Jack's injuries, went over the updated medical reports with a fine-toothed comb.

Every one of the team physicians and specialists said the same thing:

On paper, Jack was in better shape now than he had been for over a decade and with two years left on his contract, Dallas was obliged to let him attend training camp and compete for his job.

Legally they had no choice and publicly it would be a shit storm of bad press if they released or traded Jack.

Suddenly the shining legacy of the Dallas gunslinger they had invested thirty years of time and money would be for nothing if he won that all important seventh ring with another team.

So management agreed, for better or worse... Jack was back.

Worst case scenario: if he showed up to training camp and couldn't perform, they could slide him into some form of coaching role. Stick him with a tablet and keep him close.

Jack's demands going into camp were relatively simple:

First: Jack’s salary would be placed in trust with the Greene Corporation.

He didn’t need the money, let the charities have it.

Second: Jackson Greene would do no video interviews this year and wanted to play with the darkest face shield allowed for his helmet.

Pre- or post-game, it made no difference. Jack wouldn't be participating in the media circus.

And lastly, he would be wearing the darkest face shield allowed by the league. He didn't need a medical reason, he just wanted it that way.

Dallas had no problem with the money issue. They even went so far as to use it as PR by matching his salary it with a charity of his choice.

However, they didn't like the "no communication" rule until the league PR department tested it and found the fans liked the "mystery" of it all. It was only then that Dallas eventually agreed to abide by his wishes.

The League also ruled in Jackson's favor over the facial shield due in no small part to the hit he took the year before.

The talking heads took no time at all to beak out the tape from last year's conference championship injury.

The frozen look of excruciating pain on Jackson's face as his spine disintegrated flashed across every program in the system, so they figured it was perfectly natural for him to want to protect his face. Not that the league PR guys didn't have ulterior motives.

They knew it would drive the media mad and as the first pictures from training camp came rolling in the media frenzy kicked off in full.

The salivating public got a look at Jack's bearded face hidden behind a dark poly-carbon visor. He was looking lean and mean, his passes sharp off the snap, those fifty year old feet quick and agile.

Jack was back and the merchandise, season tickets, and net pass sales went through the roof and the League loved it. . Jackson Greene's sports media machine roared to life with fuel born from his re-birth.

People want to believe in miracles but love car wrecks just as much.

In Jackson Greene they had both.

Before the first snaps of the pre-season, the public could smell blood in the water. The media pumped stories about Jack's age and possible failure; splashing on the surface hoping for a shark.

The tabloids started screaming headlines like, "For a man so in love with his own face, why does he go to such lengths to hide it? One has to wonder if the scars behind the mask might be the cause behind his divorce from former supermodel Samantha Williams-Greene!"

If only the yellow sheet journalists could realize how close to the truth they really were. Only it wasn't scars he was trying to hide but the lack of them.

The youthful visage behind his visor and facial hair had become worse than any scar to Jackson.

His thick burly beard had given him back some of the lost age but the dark hair and crystal clear eyes were apparent to his teammates.

To the public and media, the guys made jokes about Jackson covering up the gray with *Just For Men* in an effort to try and look younger in order to wrangle a new pretty wife.

But behind closed doors, there were rumors in the locker room of human growth hormone, organic and bionic implants. Nobody had the guts to ask but it was till there.

Thankfully the “Big Blue Line” that was Dallas kept shit in house, where it belonged. As far as the public needed to know was Jack’s arm was strong, his feet were quick, and his vision was dead on.

Whatever deal or sacrifice he had made, the gun-slinger was back and they loved him for it.

****

The last droplets of the Blue in Vial one bit the dust four days before the season opener in Beijing and Jack put no thought into it at all.

What mattered to him now was the season.

The routine of endless hours of film study, regimented work out, and travel before game day.

He had become so used to the grinding nature of his existence that anytime the almost uncomfortable "buzz" of energy started to wane, Jackson would find a quiet place to "refuel."

The machine inside Jackson Greene fired on all cylinders and the Blue was the pure fuel that kept its hard charging pace intact.

As the season progressed, media attention on Jackson grew at an exponential rate, feeding like parasites off the secrecy he enveloped himself in.

From never removing his helmet during the games and skipping all press conferences to being whisked away in black private cars, Jack had become more like an eccentric drug-addled rock star than a world-famous athlete.

There was, however, no questioning his effectiveness on the gridiron.

He was ruthless.

A lifetime of experience packed into a jet powered version of himself, Jack could pulled off plays that had been off the Dallas books for over a decade. Week after week, the world watched as Jackson would play his heart out, leaving blood on each and every field.

He was fearless.

Smashing through men twice his size and three decades younger than him, Jack managed to give every bit much damage as he got. And yet at five a.m. every Tuesday morning, Jack would show up fresh and injury-free in the training facilities an hour before the coaching staff arrived.

His ability to bounce back from injuries sustained on game day astounded the med team. They just had no explanation for why a man his age should be able to do the things he was able to do.

Jack didn't need doctors. He wasn't afraid of the pain or the collisions.

Damn the pain.

The pain didn't matter...

His flesh was living steel, malleable under the influence of Dr. Litwinczuk's magical liquid fire. Its chaotic energy drowning away any vexing questions and hiding doubts behind an unrecognizable face.

The face of a young man in the mirror with aged eyes.

Jack wasn't afraid of anything...not anymore.

He just needed the Blue. Its warmth soothed him to sleep after Sunday's slaughters, and drove his workout madness during the week.

The world championship would be in his grasp long before they stepped foot on the field for the Conference championships at the Dallas Dome.

He had beaten his team into a fire-breathing colossus over this, the last, longest season of his career.

An entire mega-city screamed out for blood and Jackson Greene was willing to oblige.

The opposition never had a snowballs chance in Texas of standing up to the Dallas assault.

****

Vial two ran dry one week before the world championship in London and like all addicts, Jack never saw the train wreck waiting for him at the end of the track.

Juicing up on the Trans-Atlantic hop between Austin and London Jack knew exactly what the loss of that second vial meant as his hands shook from the deoxyribonucleic acid overload. The telomeres flaring to life like a burning star from the last of Doctor Litwinczuk’s liquid lightning brought tears to his eyes in the bathroom knowing it was all over.

The doctor hadn't left any instructions for the drug's use with the exception of his explicit warning to not use all three ampules.

The sincere look of caution on the Doctor's face when he warned of a life ending in terrible pain and regret stayed Jackson's hand when that comforting inner fire started to wane.

For the entire championship week, Jack was hold up in the penthouse of the team hotel in London as the inevitable moment when the drugs dry up hit and he was no different than any other junkie.

As the withdrawal from the Blue enveloped him Jackson felt like a double dose of the worst flu ever surge in on him like flood waters in a levee breach.

Sweating through five days of intense, almost psychotic depression as his body gradually adjusted to the lack of Litwinczuk's magic liquid in his system.

Jackson's could seem to do anything but sleep but found no rest as it was twisted by terrifying hallucinations.

Sometimes it was visions of himself trapped in a hospital bed; dessicated and unattended, left to rot as the machines dedicated to keeping him alive screamed in a terrifying mechanical voice for him to die.

On other nights Jack was trapped at the bottom of a crystalline vial, the old Doctor laughing down at him with his crooked yellow teeth. With shaking hands the Doc would drown Jackson in a tide of the magical blue liquid.

By his third day in country, sleep terrified Jackson to the point that he was guzzling gallons of energy drinks and handfuls of uppers to keep himself awake. Jack had been awake for two days straight before the team brought in a medical team to sedate him and keep a close eye on the situation.

When he awoke on the morning of the world championship, Jackson Greene was calm and sedate.

The madness in his eyes gone.

The paranoid rage was gone.

The pain and questioning was replaced instead with icy determination.

In the darkness of his unconscious mind, Jack had been given an answer...

****

Why?

It was always the driving force behind life, the why. And that was had been revealed to Jackson in the Darkness.

With the passing of time everything in Jackson Greene's life had become a question of why.

Why risk everything for something you have already done?

Why not be satisfied with the legacy one has earned?

"Why" was what Samantha had asked him a thousand times, her dark almond eyes sparkling with tears. "Why throw your life away on moment in times that can never be recreated?"

And, after he had destroyed it all, the universe had given Jackson had been given a second chance at life. To start over and create something new out of a life wasted and what did he do with it?

He threw himself back into the meat grinder for no other reason than he could.

That was what the dark had shown him. It had revealed all those beautiful moments over a lifetime of dedication to the gladiatorial life.

From the joy of tossing the pigskin with a father long since gone to those quiet moments of reflection after a loss, they were all precious to him.

Jack had been a terrible husband and father but he was an extraordinary football player.

Running out on the field tonight; adrenaline rushing and blood pumping through his brain filled with fear, Jackson Greene found the taste in his mouth was sweet. As sweet as the first time he ever stepped on a field

Sitting back in his locker while billions of eyes across the system waiting for him to rush back out on to the field, Jackson knew he didn't need the Blue.

All Jack needed was to remember "why."

Standing up slowly, Jackson's pulse began to race as he moved to follow his teammates up the tunnel.

Marching back up the tunnel and back into the fray, the sound of half a million voices thundered down the concrete pipe; battering Jack's ear drums and filling his soul with pride.

Jackson Greene's why was simple.

"Because this is who I am..."

Private
Garden

Private Garden

H1, or Heliah One is a delicate, twinkling blue jewel dancing around the triple stars of Alpha Centauri A-B and Proxima Centauri. It takes more than four years for light from our sun to show as a twinkle in its nighttime skies.

Heliah One is also the best shot for long term human survival in the universe. Universally recognized as a fresh start in a universe not known for such generosity; mankind could not ignore the existence of such a paradise out amongst the stars.

No more domes or airlocks, low air pressure packs or gallons of UV repellent. Just a man's face bare beneath a wide open night's sky. Of the hundreds of worlds documented in humanity's journey into the void, Heliah One is by far their best chance for colonization.

So man rushed forward to expand our influence beyond the safe confines of own solar system.

Trillions of credits were pumped into scientific studies across the system as every mind with a doctorate tried to crack secrets long since relegated to science fiction.

Long term hibernation was far too dangerous, no one could withstand that length of time floating away in the deep.

Besides which, nothing large enough to care the fuel required for a journey of that length had ever been imagined. So humanity turned their desperate eyes to the last long-shot in the race: F.T.L. or Faster Than Light powered space craft.

At the end of the world the term F.T.L. began to be bantered about in boardrooms and living rooms alike.

Once considered the folly of madmen and fools alike, F.T.L. theories buried in ancient yellowed papers of museums world wide suddenly got a second and sometimes third look as the future stared everyone in the face.

As if the work of two hundred years of theoretical physics could be suddenly overturned just because we needed it to.

Humanity wanted, no, *needed* to plant their flags on this far away piece of the universe.

Greedy hands wrung in anticipation of its boundless resources and wide open spaces while the ordinary man just dreamed of a world to raise his children in that actually had a real future.

But isn't that the way it always seems to work? Greed and fear working hand in hand?

With the extraordinary colonial successes of Lunar One on the Moon in 2155 and Oasis Two, or "Mars Dome" in 2168, the deep space research field had more patrons now than during the Age of Explorers back in the fifteenth century.

The patrons in this new age of colonization were the mega-conglomerates: companies like EnerCorp, Agri-Nation, and Medi-Pharm.

Industrial concerns so large that their influence was found in every part of ordinary life.

With massive corporate coffers that were deep and cavernous, it was only naturally their influence would spread beyond the Rim when it was their gold that paid for the discoveries that made it all scientifically possible.

While there was enough pieces of pie for everyone, it was Enercorp that was awarded the lions' share of major contracts. From construction of deep space vehicles as well as the F.T.L. propulsion systems to the long term Terra-forming plans for Heliah One, it would take the Houston based industrial giant more than a million man hours to work out the details.

With EnerCorp planning out the logistics behind outfitting, training, and transporting work crews; it was no surprise inter-company cannibalism would end up filling a majority of the most lucrative positions within the Heliah Colonization Expedition.

It was this corporate nepotism that brought Masterson Fawkes to an early morning meeting after pulling graveyard shifts for almost a month. Barely able to keep his eyes open, trying desperately to make love to a cup of coffee, Fawkes grumped silently in his head.

It's my day off... I'm not even supposed to be here today.

Up till this morning, Fawkes was the ranking supervisor at EnerCorp's Oxygen Reclamation plant in Baja, New California. All that title really meant was he kept a small army of klinking-klanking robots from locking down in the harsh sun and salt-water bath of the inland sea. People were not his strong suit and at this moment it took everything inside him not to walk out on the “opportunity of a lifetime” for some much need sleep.

“Fawkes... I can call you Fawkes, right? You should feel lucky to get off this damn planet. Who wouldn't want a fresh start, free of all the problems?”

Flown in from corporate in Houston, the suit was definitely a pro. A heavy hitting recruiter brought in with a picture perfect pitch to make the sale.

“Why should you continue to kill yourself every day trying to make it in a world of absolute minimums?

Really? You're asking me why? Look around you brother...

Fawkes only thought it, knowing if he said anything out loud instead of just smiling and sipping his coffee would extend the meeting even longer.

Ever since a random asteroid strike by UE34 wasted the majority of the South American rain forests, reclamation of oxygen and conservation of resources had become a planet wide priority.

Each year, rigs like this one helped to put more than a billion liters of oxygen back into the atmosphere by breaking down the rising sea water from global warming into its essential elemental components. Reclamation plants combined the harvested oxygen with nitrogen to match atmospheric needs while capturing the hydrogen for fuel usage. Absolutely nothing goes to waste on the planet now.

Earth was trying to teach humanity something but sadly most just seemed to miss the message.

Folks live like they don’t notice the insanity of living on a planet where one can suffocate just by walking out into the sunshine on a beautiful summer’s day.

Fawkes blamed the apathy on assholes like the pitch-man sitting across from him.

From the rumpled, sweat-stained, designer shirt to his flushed face glistening with sweat from the short walk up the stairs to Fawkes' office, “Mr. Closer” here was an exemplary example of what was wrong with the humanity.

This man would surely die on a trip out to one of the big rigs during a tropical storm and yet he couldn't live without it? He couldn’t relate to what really made life on the planet possible for guys like him.

There was no chance he’d be exposed to radiation while changing out a 200mW engine on a high velocity wind turbine.

Nor would he fear explosive decompression digging for rare earth elements 4000 meters below the waves. His soft hands were destined for a lifetime of tapping on a keyboard.

A century's worth of over saturation in instant gratification had become ingrained in humanity's DNA, and it is this unreasonable expectation that caused mankind's disconnect from the realities of life on Earth.

Fawkes stared across the desk with derision as the pitchman continued on with his bill of sale.

" Let's not even mention about the adventure, Fawkes! For over a decade you have shown your dedication and worth on the oxygen reclamation and desalinization rigs here in the Gulf of Baja, let us reward you..."

Patting a sheen of sweat from his brow with a handkerchief, the closer shifting in his seat to pull out a contract tablet from his satchel, laying it between them on the desk.

“It has been decided back in Houston that you should be rewarded for your passion and commitment as a first tier asset to the company. You are officially on the top of our “short list” for first stage of colonization on Heliah One.”

Fawkes was momentarily taken a back by the offer, scanning through the contract addendum to hide his surprise. This did not stop the pitchman from continuing his best barker routine.

The man could smell the sale a shark smells blood in the water.

“Heavy-duty construction is scheduled for nearly twenty years, so it will be a long time before the first colonist ever steps off a deep-space liner on Heliah One.

“By that time, you and your crews will have long since made it through the construction phase, and with the luxurious retirement Enercorp is willing to guarantee in your new extended contract,”

The suit leaned back in his chair, extrending his hands so the holo-projectors in his cuffs would kick in behind him. Suddenly the entire office wall lit up with a colorful holographic rendition of the final commercial plans for Heliah One.

"You will be living like a king! "

Blue green waters glittering like the most perfect piece of glass touched by the soft white sandy beaches. Beautiful mountain chalets with snow dappled, chocolate brown roofs hidden away in waiting mountain passes.

Fawkes had to admit it did looked like paradise.

"Just think about it. A million in credits and land ownership rights added to your normal retirement package....I'd call that a real life of luxury.

"All of it just waiting for you to sign the contract." and with that the pitchman sat back with nothing left in the arsenal.

The huckster knew if the hologram and bonuses didn't sell it, nothing would.

His eyes glittering like a predator, he asked the ultimate question, "What have you got to lose?"

It's a simple choice to you isn't it? All you want from us is to travel halfway across the galaxy, grow algae in the water, pump oxygen into the atmosphere and reshape an entire planet.

Yeah, a life of luxury awaits... If we survive. If we survive the sub-zero winters and tropical summers.

If we survive the colossal construction projects or all the statistically probable disasters that could strike the colony down in its entirety.

"If" is an awful big word to gamble on when your life is on the line.

It was that line of thinking that stopped Fawkes cold in his place. If survival was the only obstacle standing between him and the "good" life than what the hell was even thinking about?

Fawkes hadn't known anything but the struggle for survival in his thirty five years on the planet and what the fuck did he have left on Earth that was worth hanging onto?

Out on the rigs for weeks at a time trying to save a dying planet. No wife, no kids. A ratty little apartment that even the cockroaches wouldn't touch.

The pitchman had Fawkes dead to right so he pressed his thumb to the tablet and signed up to take the job.

Like his Daddy used to say, "Sometimes boy, you've just gotta' roll the bones and hope for a seven."

Fawkes signed the contract.

*

The official "Bon Voyage" party for the Heliah Colonization Expedition roared long into the night beneath Mars Dome as thousands of revelers celebrated humanity's greatest moment in history.

A chaotic storm of party goers joining with their heroes in one last frenzy before launch. From the observation bridge leading to the H.C.E. shuttle bays, the twinkling lights of neon colored phosphorescent dancers mingled amongst the flash of cameras, sparkling like stars in the wide open park below.

And lost in the middle of in of it was Masterson Fawkes.

In the twenty-two weeks of psychological scrutiny and excruciating training at Star City in KAZAKHSTAN, they could teach a man how to stay calm long enough to get rescued if separated from his spacecraft.

Unfortunately, there was no cosmonaut training for how to prepare a man for that moment when the whole world is watching.

Only one of thousands of H.C.E. crew members mingling in the midsts of a roaring, human hurricane of attention, Fawkes' natural urge was to shrink among the violets and escape the attention.

Fresh off the hardest challenge of his life, the flood of alcoholic sweet drinks and neon glowing dancers were almost alien compared to the utilitarian meals and technological tortures back in Star City.

The Russians in charge of the H.C.E. training had a century of experience in successful space travel and were as hard as iron at the same time cold as ice. Fawkes could still see the bear of man in charge of his training class walking the line, bald head shining like polished metal as he ground down the weak and ill-prepared.

“The only way to train a man for terrors of Big Black is show no mercy! Will she have mercy on you? NYET! So, neither shall I!”

For days at a time, with little sleep and the barest of creature comforts, their cosmonaut masters would prepare the cadets for possible hardships unique to their long journey ahead.

Fawkes swore up and down they spent every night dreaming of the most insane "training"their vodka fueled minds could come up with just to torture him with.

Perhaps those frozen nights in Kazakhstan had left him with a touch of post traumatic stress syndrome as he stood there, body shivering unconsciously from the thought of being trapped all alone in the dark.

Submerged beneath a hundred feet of water, trying desperately to restore power and life support to his survival pod. Fawkes could only hope everything the Russians had put him through was worth the nightmares.

At this moment none of that training mattered.

Being in the middle of the largest media frenzy to ever hit the system left Fawkes with the urgent need to escape from the madness and cacophony.

Walking quickly through the overwhelming crowd, engulfed by blinding camera flashes Masterson moved forward through the mass of humanity between him and the shuttle bays.

Gentle hands tugging at his flight suit, Fawkes rebuffed the attention of eager revelers hoping to keep him there with them with the reward of a kiss or perhaps more. Glowing, anonymous beauties plying their flights of fancy, they couldn't possibly know it was far too late to bring out the joy in Masterson Fawkes .

By the time he made it to the security station on the loading arch, sweat was pouring down his face as a full on panic attack roared to life, freezing him in place directly above the joyous fray below. Holding on to the railing with a white-knuckled grip, Fawkes tried desperately to block the insanity below from his mind.

Struggling to catch his breath, Fawkes leaned back his head and stared straight up into the face of his impending future floating gently above Mars Dome.

Dunstan and *Anne*.

Two of the largest starships ever conceived, they were mammoth in scale, literally blocking out the view of space throught the dome.

Dunstan's giant delta wing, its bright white nano-carbon infused skin dwarfing the more traditionally long and thin industrial piston form of *Anne*.

Surrounded by the twinkling firefly lights of much smaller craft making last minute deliveries during the preparations for launch, making the two of them appear to be planets onto themselves.

They truly are the Wonders of all worlds, Fawkes thought n the shadow of their greatness, he could feel the tension of being in the midst of the maelstrom slowly dissipate.

**

Seriously twisted off from a half dozen novelty sized piña coladas, Eleanor “Deck” Fillian sat on a wobbly bar stool trying to figure out why she couldn't relax and just enjoy the moment.

Deck worked her whole life for an opportunity like this one. Graduating top of the class at Academy, ten years piloting long range transports from the rim and commercial space, she was more than qualified for this assignment.

So the question had to be asked: Why was she sitting by herself in this back-door bar completely shit faced on the eve of the greatest astronautically significant flight in the history of humanity.

Deck had no idea. What she did know; after catching glimpse of her sullen, blood-shot eyes in the mirror behind the bar, is that it was time to wrap things up or this drunk was going to turn into a funk real quick.

Pushing away her over-sized glass with the remains of its fruity drink, Deck reached across the bar to snatch a shot of bourbon from a bottle left unattended in the madness.

The sweet burn slipped down her throat quickly, numbing her nerves while fueling the fire in her belly.

Placing the bourbon back behind the mahogany bar, Deck grabbed an unsliced orange that lay waiting to be carved up before plunging out into the chaos.

The crowd was right on the hairy edge, inching closer and closer to being out of control, made clear by the large contingents of security scattered liberally through the masses.

Knowing the H.C.E. wouldn't look kindly on a flight officer getting thrown in the brig less than twenty-four hours from launch, Deck moved quickly through the crowd and towards the loading arch.

Avoiding loosely handled drinks and groping strangers with the skill only a pilot retains regardless of their state of inebriation, the nervous apprehension started to creep free of the rum and bourbon fueled fire in her guts.

Could it really be the damn mission that was causing her nervous apprehension?

Was it pre-flight jitters? She had spent more than her fair share on long runs but nothing like what they were about to attempt.

Five years riding the edge of an energy wave, traveling just a few tick-tocks this side of the speed of light, Deck was about to crew the longest deep-space journey ever attempted by humanity and up until this evening never had a single moment of doubt.

If everything worked out right, she would be back in orbit over Mars Dome in a little less than a decade. Flush with enough credits in her account to buy up a freighter of her own and leave the dregs of contract work behind, on paper this was a win-win situation.

Even the sickening thought of what would happen if things went wrong that had didn't bother her.

Yeah, she would have to hitch a ride on *Anne* for the return flight to Mars, which equaled cold storage for nearly two decades. Every person she ever knew would be old and gray by the time Deck got back but she would be twice as rich.

Accident and hazard pay was double and thoughts of being wealthy would always trump the fear of dying in her mind when death is the absolute worst case scenario. Deck had long believed that death was unavoidable; a variable one had to easily ignore if they wanted to actually have a life.

Mortality held little sway in the manner to which she lived.

Stopped momentarily at the security checkpoint, Deck stared up at *Dunstan* and *Anne* floating gently above her in the night sky. In the face of her destiny Eleanor "Deck" Fillian felt her calm confidence return. She was suddenly energized, washed free of the doubt and ready for the journey ahead.

This was going to be the greatest adventure of her life. Her name would go down in the annals of history with the greats like Sally Ride, John Glenn, Neil Armstrong so why not enjoy it? She knew, just like those heroes who had come before her, that with any great adventure there will come pitfalls and dangers.

The key was owning the fear of the unknown.

So Deck screamed out at the raucous crowd below, her voice joining theirs in a joyous chorus of sound. The primordial part of her soul calling out to the dark with a million other voices, celebrating life with a rapture that was almost orgasmic.

With life reaffirmed and a semi-intoxicated smile back on her lips, Deck started toward the waiting shuttle when she caught glimpse of a tall drink of water standing all alone in his light blue jumpsuit.

Clutching at the arch railing, staring silently up at *Dunstan*, the scruffy roughneck almost seemed lost in madness around him

Interesting... perhaps there's still time left to celebrate, she thought to herself.

Tossing the orange up and down in her right hand, Deck watched the handsome stranger collect himself before following him down into the shuttle loading zone.

***

There is a moment, usually within seconds of waking from a night of heavy carousing that one has to questions the decisions of the evening before. Whether it be from the physical pain from over indulging or a strange warm body laying next to you in bed, life has a tendency to clue one in quickly to the consequences of impulsive decisions.

The lingering scent of jasmine and citrus on his sheets the morning of launch was Fawkes' clue.

Struggling to shake free the remnants of glowing sweet drinks that fogged up his brain, it was a long, dried out orange peel in beneath the pillow that brought the memories of the night before to surface.

Having finally caught his breath, Fawkes felt his bullish heartbeat calm while walking through the airlock for the virtually empty shuttle trip back to *Dunstan.*

Here and there sat a tired, worn out face with a look of resignation resting in the seats. Each soul exhausted despite the desperate need to carry on the celebration.

Belting in to his seat, Fawkes sat back and closed his eyes. The comforting ozone-like smell of heavily recycled air and sound proofing ensured silence was working their magic, quickly lulling him into nap mode.

His eyelids grew heavy, sleep's slow hand drifting over his mind the citrusy smell of a peeled orange drifted into Fawkes' nostrils.

The sound of hands tearing at its skin, teeth noisily eating the tangy guts followed the scent driving rest back into the shadows and forcing him to open his eyes.

Turning his head to catch glimpse of his noisy neighbor, Fawkes knew he had opened a whole case of trouble when the fiery haired, little rocket jockey turned her diminutive frame in the seat to stare back at him.

Waiting patiently for a few minutes, the ol' roughneck stared off into the darkness, hoping she would loose interest.

It quickly became apparent she wasn't going any where as she went about eating the orange without shifting in her seat.

"You look nervous." Deck asked, her eyes twinkled up at Fawkes in the dim cabin light as an effortless smile crossed her face.

Feigning grumpiness, Fawkes responded flippantly to her observation, "I'm Masterson Fawkes. How the hell are you?"

Trying to stay irritated at having his nap ruined which was quite a chore as she continued to smile that beautiful but dangerously crooked little grin. Holding out her petite, orange coated hand to shake, she finally introduced herself.

"I'm Eleanor Fillian but everybody calls me Deck."

"Deck?" Fawkes asked, wiping off his now-sticky hand on the leg of his flight suit.

"Short for '*Hit The*.' I've always had a tendency to stick with a problem way longer than is probably safe, so if I'm running away it's time to--"

"Hit the deck, I get it," he chuckled at her morbid humor.

"So what's the story Fawkes, not a big fan of crowds?"

"Not really..." his smile fading quickly.

Deck could see Fawkes was hiding something but what was the point of digging at the past?

Besides she liked it when the scruffy roughneck smiled, so she shifted gears and let it go.

"Bullshit. Having a moment of deep space regret were we? Afraid the whole thing will explode and you'll get the choice of frozen death or burning death?" Deck could hardly believe she had actually said it, even as the words left her lips.

She was coming on in that weird, awkward way that only works on may be one guy in ten and generally, creeps the average man out to the point of conversation death.

Fawkes just gave her quick knowing smile, acknowledging the essential truth of her joke without actually making a sound.

Deck pulled her legs up into the chair, putting the mangled orange down in her lap for a moment to place her sticky hands on Fawkes forearm.

“Not that you should worry about that. In fact, I think death in any form should be the least of your worries.”

“And why is that?” Fawkes asked, becoming intoxicated by this beautiful woman's touch and attention. Here they were, on the edge of the universe, ready to jump off the edge into the abyss and she was working so hard to make him smile.

Deck stared deep into Fawkes' eyes with an almost hypnotic gaze as she answered.

"Well... the particle acceleration drives aboard *Dunstan* haven't been deep space tested yet. Who knows what might happen? We might put the pedal to the metal and *poof*! We're all cotton candy headed for someone's mouth."

"And what exactly is the probability of cotton candy transmogrification?" he asked, sliding over in his seat, trying to inch as close to her as he could.

Rising up on her knees, Deck whispered into his ear, ".0000042 percent" before passionately kissing Fawkes with citrus and bourbon imbued lips.

****

Passion and pilots go hand in hand. It was a part of her nature that Deck had accepted a long time ago, acknowledging that it would cause problems every once in a while.

The problem this morning was she couldn't figure out if she had a problem.

Yeah, coming on to that roughneck refinery guy was an impetuous decision, even in the best light. To go back to his cabin, and pass out cold without ever getting his flight suit unzipped... That was a crime.

Maybe it was a good thing she passed out. Waking up, held firmly in his warm embrace while both of them were still dressed showed the grease monkey could at least control himself. Masterson Fawkes was a strange sort, or at least from what Deck could remember of the conversation in between their passionate kisses.

Not that they had any deep intellectual meeting of minds. She kinda landed that bird hot on the launchpad by kissing him first.

No. It was something in the way his body reacted to her touch.

Almost as if Fawkes were aching for the contact of another human being but not having any idea how to get it. Or she was really shit-faced and horny, imagining a connection in the bourbon enhanced passion of the moment.

Either way, the look of peace on his Masterson's face when Deck awoke was enough to make her want to find out if he was a problem or opportunity.

It wasn't like she was worried that getting involved with the roughneck would some how affect her career. The company didn't frown on fraternization.

Hell, most of the humans in the system worked for one of maybe six companies, it would be harder to date somebody who wasn't employed by the same company.

Laying back on her pillow soft bunk, Deck hoped some quiet time would lead to perspective. He had to show up in her life when she should have been steely edged. This was the greatest flight of her life and all she could think about was Masterson Fawkes.

*****

Fawkes hung two hundred feet in the air, fighting magnetic suspension cables while trying to lock down an errant piece of equipment the size of a shuttle craft. Covered in thick amber-colored grease, struggling to synchronize the couplings, his mind wasn't really on the task at hand.

It kept drifted back to her.

The sweet gentle breath of Deck sleeping on his chest lingered gently in his thoughts.

It had been a long time since Fawkes had felt the comforting warmth of another soul help sooth him to sleep and the distraction of having her in his mind quickly became dangerous.

When Masterson missed the sound of a proximity alarm from one his little robo-helpers, it only took a single slap from one of the ten tonne greased piston shafts to bring him back to reality.

Far below, the human crew gave a collected hoot of oohs and chuckles at his rookie mistake from the cargo bay deck.

Head ringing from the collision, Fawkes momentarily felt like a punch drunk fighter from the impact. Even after recovering, and getting the cables lined up, he couldn't drive Deck Fillian from his mind.

Masterson was certain she would have laughed maniacally at him for getting beaned by that errant piston.

Witty and passionate, Deck was many things but what attracted Fawkes the most was the weird. Weird but in a deliciously wrong way, like laughing at man being bounced about because he was too stupid to put a woman out of his mind and get back to work.

What was it about meeting exactly the right person at the wrong time? Wasn't that one of Murphy's laws? Fawkes was certain he had read that somewhere.

With everything finally back in its place, and no other last minute emergencies to take up their time, Fawkes let the crew off to settle in before the launch.

Slapping his team on the back, he knew they planned on congregating in the common area of the ship but had no intention of joining their get together.

Nope, there was just enough time for a shower and find Deck before launch.

******

One of the most interesting innovations of the H.C.E. *Dunstan* was in the way it was designed to accommodate both crew and cargo.

Being essentially a flying wind, a design dating back to the beginnings of manned flight, Dunstan looked like a single form spacecraft the size of old Manhattan Island.

In reality, she was intricately compartmentalized, with four gigantic living compartments know as Emergency Environmental Pods, or EPods, flush mounted along the bottom of her massive wing structure.

Constructed as long term housing for the crews on Heliah, each E-Pod was its own habitat with a small nuclear reactor as a power source and independent set of flight controls. Designed to stand in as an emergency escape vehicles as well, each E-Pod was a perfectly capable deep space vessel on its own.

As part of the command crew for EPod One, Deck had access to every part of this ship. Sliding her lithe fingers across the security panel for Masterson Fawkes' quarters, the lock click open in response to her flight command status. Smiling a naughty grin, Deck slipped inside quickly.

Pod One wasn't scheduled for cryo-sleep for another year. There was plenty of time for them to get to know each other before their stasis cycle but she just wanted touch his sun kissed skin. The chemistry of attraction from firing off every synapse in her brain when it came to Masterson Fawkes.

She wanted to hear him talk.

Enjoy that slip of a southern accent in his voice.

To feel that sandpaper-like beard rub against the back of her neck as he leaned down to plant his lips on her shoulder. Just the thoughts cause Deck to shivered with delight as she stepped into his quarters.

Having kept track off him via the on-board monitoring system, she had caught his dance with the ten tonne piece of metal in the cargo bay. The mess it made of him was truly funny, once Deck could see he was alright.

As the door shut silently behind her, she knew exactly where she was and exactly what she was doing, until the hum of the vibro-shower suddenly stopped and Fawkes walked out naked with a curious smile on his face.

“Commander Fillian,” Fawkes took his time walking over and putting on the fresh blue jumpsuit that was laid out on his bed. “Did someone report a problem with my shower?”

Taking a seat, Deck tried to show no surprise by Fawkes bare flesh, never turning her gaze. She had traveled more than a million flight hours trapped in tin cans with a battalion of denuded men but this time she was truly thankful inside for this long look.

"Are you really gonna stay in this gloomy room during the launch?"

"Why do you have a better option?" Fawkes asked as he sat down on his bunk directly opposite Deck; slipping on his jumpsuit and lightly magnetized shoes that was the off duty uniform.

Deck hoping over to his bunk, sitting so close to Fawkes that he could smell the sweet mix of her sweat and a long lingering perfume she had put on hours before.

Leaning in close, she whispered in his ears, "You've never had better company."

Wrapping his strong hands around the small of her back, Fawkes pulled Deck so close she could feel the ambient heat of his body burning against her chest. His delicious whiskers tickling her cheek as she leaned into his embrace...

" You not wrong there pretty lady. "

Rewarded him with a gentle kiss on his rock solid jaw, Deck sprang up from the bunk and Fawkes' eager grasp.

Backing slowly towards the door, Deck opening it with a quick swipe of her hand before flashing Fawkes that wicked grin of hers before asking, "You coming with me or not?"

"Are you coming.... Are you kidding me?" Fawkes rose quickly to follow her out into the hall.

****

If there is one scientific constant in the universe, it is: Two people falling in love cannot hide it from the world around them.

Not that Deck or Fawkes were contemplating the realities of falling in love at this moment.

Right now they were like random magnetic forces stuck in each other's orbit; each eagerly chasing the other around until that inevitable moment when they meet and change everything forever.

Fawkes' crew, already well into their cups before seeing the Chief come in, knew from months of training back at Star City that his brooding and serious attitude was a natural state.

Yet there he was, all chatty and smiling, hanging on Deck's every word.

This sight, even if it was a moment of random joy fed their collective spirits. A good omen to these celestial sailors if there ever was one.

It managed to raise the morale of the crew higher than it had been in months before the two of them took leave of the commons.

Smiles and full glasses were raised to the Chief's luck as they continuing on their meandering adventure together.

Deck was magnetic, and Fawkes was completely lost in her presence. Even the most inane topics seemed to led to deep thoughtful conversations while miles of halls and corridors passed beneath their feet.

Time flew by as they wandered about the guts of H.C.E. *Dunstan*. He hardly noticed when they crossed over into the secured flight control area for E-Pod One.

It wasn't until a massive set of doors block their path and Deck was momentarily surrounded by the red lights of the biometric scanners did Fawkes figure it out.

Quickly verifying her identity, the shining sealed doors in front of them cracked open. The hushed release of vacume sealed air tossing both their hair gently.

Turning back to Fawkes, Deck backed slowly into the room, giving him with a gentle but challenging gaze. The further in she moved the more lights around her flickered to life, designed to react to the physical presence of flight crew.

Wandering over to the cabin length observation window, Masterson was entranced by the lights of Oasis dome glittering like a diamond below them.

"Uhhh....Are we supposed to be in here?" he asked quizzically, not sure whether his presence on the flight deck was up to regs.

"Sure we are," Deck replied, playfully pushing Fawkes with a gentle hand on his lower back towards the observation window seating. "Or at least I am.

"You they might shoot for trespassing."

With a gentle wave of her hands, the console directly behind Fawkes flared to life. "Now, stay quiet." Deck whispered before taking her place in the command chair.

Watching the storm of numbers stream together, flowing from one piece of the liquid console glass to another under Deck's orchestration, Masterson Fawkes was taken aback by the beauty of the moment.

Synchronizing quickly with the rest of *Dunstan's* systems, Deck frenetically manipulating the data on the screens. E-Pod One was online and prepared for the jump before she called out for a communications check, "Comms are up and online, do you read *Dunstan* Actual?"

The screen lit up with color as the image of Captain David Bonney quickly came into focus. His red hair full and thick, barely singed by silver, he looked immaculate for a man of sixty five. His navy blues were immaculate, chest festooned with the colorful ribbons of a man who had sacrificed his entire life to the service.

A military man through and through, Captain Bonney had believed so much in this mission he resigned his command of the battle-wagon *Atlantica* along with a forty year career in Interstellar Navy. All just to lead the H.C.E. mission.

"To cross the great abyss," as he put it, "would be humanity's greatest accomplishment and I will be at the helm."

Despite having only met the man briefly during orientation at Star City, Fawkes was truly inspired by the rugged commander and his zealous attitude towards this mission. Captain David Bonney was a man cut from the cloth of the old world.

You knew when he said something, it was written in stone. He was a man to be trusted.

A rare smile rested on the old sailor's face, when the Captain responded. "Roger that, Lieutenant Fillian. Good to have you on the comm. How are things down in E-Pod One? Everything up here reads good to go."

"We are clean and green across the board, sir. Observation dome closed and locked, emergency engines online. We are sealed up tighter than a bullfrog's ass, Captain."

"Good work, Deck. We have a hot clock of T-minus 30 minutes and counting. Stay close to the board and let us know if anything jumps out of place before launch. Dunstan actual, out."

"Roger that, Captain, EP One out."

Deck came down to the observation seats, standing close to Fawkes as *Dunstan* made its way out of orbit above Mars Dome. "Did you know that the ruling corporate board for the H.C.E. decided the trip aboard *Dunstan*, with its experimental particle acceleration drive, was deemed far too dangerous for the transfer of plant and animal life samples destined for Heliah One?

Deck pointed out the glowing pipe that was *Anne* hanging off their starboard bow when she came into view. “In that one decision, the construction of *Anne* was suddenly required and the entire project was delayed almost five years.”

Watching as her massive rotating habitat pods turned in a perpetual circle around the main body of the spacecraft, it made sense to Fawkes. Anne was a gargantuan zoological and biological habitat and her deep space design had been in service for nearly a half a century.

It was tried and true technology. A virual ark of DNA as well as a selection of naturally adaptive species in hiber-sleep was in her care and Anne would protect every plant and creature that was to be transplanted to Heliah One safely. The trailblazing part of this mission would be left to Dunstan, her cargo of muscle and steel easy commodities to replace if something were to go wrong midflight.

“I'm actually surprised it took humanity this long to get here....” Deck whispered as she took Fawkes' hand in hers, smiling up at his rugged profile. “The question of whether fast as light travel was never ‘could it be done’ but ‘how do you carry enough fuel to do it with?’”

Leading him over to the observation window, Deck pointed to the titanium airfoils along the edges of her wing shaped frame.

“ Dunstan is special because her engines work on the combustion of anti-hydrogen and hydrogen, which only occurs when you introduce a very small amount of hydrogen into a containment chamber filled with anti-hydrogen.

“The energy released from this particle level explosion is significantly powerful enough to push us to the very edge of the speed of light.

"So the question was, how does one collect anti-hydrogen in high enough levels to make a trip like ours time manageable? The answer lie in those airfoils. Once the particle accelerator, at the heart of *Dunstan,* reaches critical mass, it will cause a spatial disruption all along our bow--"

"Whoa.... Seriously?" Fawkes was a smart guy, graduating in the top fifty of his class in college, and even lost in what Deck was trying to explain, he knew what the words *spatial disruption* meant.

"Nobody said anything about black holes when I signed up for this trip."

"Well, my dear Mr. Fawkes," Deck nearly laughed out loud at the moment of panic that came over his face. "I know who slept through their flight engineering training at Star City. It was explained in detail then that these are not black holes. It is an anti-matter bubble."

Bubble? Black hole? Fawkes pondered the difference for a moment. Super-conductive magnetics, anti-hydrogen explosion chambers, particle acceleration bubbles, semi-stable wormholes?

The whole process made Fawkes' mind swim but he knew with certainty that the press would eat H.C.E. and EnerCorp for breakfast if they knew the company was going to blast a hole in the very fabric of the universe right above Mars Dome and twenty million citizens.

Letting go of Fawkes, Deck used her hands to illustrate her point, "See, the bubble opens up a small fissure between antimatter and matter in space, like diving between temperature zones in the ocean or atmospheres when flying on earth.

The super-magnetized titanium containment traps form scoops on the front edges of the airfoils capture the antimatter and separates the anti-hydrogen from everything else.

"We are clean and green across the board, sir. Observation dome closed and locked, emergency engines are online. EP One is sealed up tighter than a bullfrog's ass, Captain."

"The containment foils then tunnel the anti-hydrogen magnetically back into the combustion chambers of old *Dunstan* here for fuel and release the rest from the containment traps at the rear.

"Thus collapsing the back edge of said bubble, giving us an almost unlimited amount of fuel for our long journey across the big black."

A beep caught Deck's attention, as last minute details from *Dunstan* Actual came in pre-launch. The countdown to launch had approached one minute as the entire ship began to vibrate.

Somewhere deep in the heart of *Dunstan*, billions of particles began dancing their excited kinetic ballet through her particle acceleration drive. The power generators controlling her magnetic capture grid increasing to maximum with a steady hum.

Ringing out over the internal comm system, Captain Bonney's voice gently warned the crew of the upcoming jump, "We are T-Minus 60 seconds from engine burn, people. All civilian personnel please prepare for launch. All flight and engineering personnel to active duty stations."

"You better buckle in up there, Fawkes," Deck warned as she strapped in to the command chair behind the console, watching the hurricane of mathematics intently. "They say the initial jump is a motherfucker but smooth sailing after that."

Sitting down in one of the observation chairs, Fawkes strapped in tightly, his nerves tense as a massive display of energy flared to life on the flight edges of *Dunstan*. A fiery storm of accelerated molecules streamed through the magnetized titanium containment traps along all the lift edges of the ship, filling the bridge of EPod One with the brightest light Fawkes had ever seen.

The captain's voice was clear as a bell as he counted down to main engine start, "T-minus 10, 9, 8, 7, 6, 5...."

Forming off their port side, Fawkes could clearly see the very fabric of space split like a jagged edge of cloth.

The place between matter and antimatter forming a darkened grotesque smile into which the universe was prepared to swallow them whole.

"4, 3, 2, 1...."

"Engaging anti-hydrogen engines!" I heard Deck yell just as the world blurred. Reality was suddenly drained of all its textures, shapes, and shades. Fawkes was acutely aware of his own existence in an absence of everything, completely unable to interact with anything.

Then just as quickly, reality snapped back into place like a picture in a slide-show, and Fawkes suddenly was back in his chair staring out the observation window on EPod One.

Shaking her head from side to side, Deck unstrapped from the command chair, looked over at Fawkes and smiled, "I told you that first step was a bitch didn't I?"

"Man, you weren't joking," pain sizzling through his brain like an anti-matter fueled ice cream headache.

"All *Dunstan* Crew!" Captain Bonney came back on the comm, overjoyed at our successful launch, the excitement apparent in his voice.

"Congratulations on being the first humans to travel as fast as light. Momentum is increasing and we should make our optimum course window in four hours.

"Stage one hibernation will commence in four hours, all civilians in hibernation group one please report to medical.

"Thank you all for the good work, people! Now let's stay vigilant and make it to our destination in one piece."

Unstrapping himself, Fawkes stood up and walked closer to the window, straightway noticing the lack of light around *Dunstan*.

No stars, no planets, just a void, deep dark and foreboding. The giant burning triangle of *Dunstan*'s airfoils did nothing to add any warmth to the depths of frozen space as our massive ship screamed through the abyss.

"It's an illusion," Deck must have seen the confused look on his face reflected in the glass, guessing what Fawkes was thinking as she walked up behind him and wrapped her arms tightly around his waist.

“The lack of light; it’s an illusion. We are moving as fast as the light of all the stars around us, so it never has the time to catch up with us. Everything is still out there; we just won’t see it till we slip back into sub-light speed.”

“So if everything is still out there, what is stopping us from plowing into a spacial object?” Fawkes asked.

“Our course computer is capable of making over a billion statistical computations in micro-seconds, and essentially keeps us clear of anything big that might come into the flight path. Besides if we were to hit anything smaller than a planet at our speed it won’t feel like anything more than turbulence.”

Turning Fawkes to face her with a quick twist of his hips, Deck reached up and pulled his face down to hers. Deck's lips mere inches from his, her hot sweet breath on Fawkes lips as she whispered,

"Basic physics, my dear Fawkes. The object with the most momentum will win in a physical fight." Deck's kiss was hard and rough, her blood obviously still pumping from the extraordinary event unfolding in front of them.

Behind them the sealed operations door slid open, Deck's replacement coming in with a cheery smile and wave. Instantaneously feeling his face flush, the junior flight officer was certain he had just interrupted a precious, private moment by checking in early for his shift.

Breaking free of their embrace, Deck turned back to the command console and the waiting red faced flight officer.

Quickly bringing him up to speed on the details of the launch, Fawkes went back to staring out into the dark void.

He had barely caught its glimmer in the observation window before a ghostly arm of plasma reached out from the void and bore down on *Dunstan* with knife-like quickness.

Ripping through *Dunstan* forward of the command bridge, the wave of liquid energy collapsed the anti-matter containment field with a giant wave of electric fire.

Tearing the great ship like paper, the air instantaneously filled with the scream of over-torqued metal and escaping oxygen.

Surging and searing its way through the engineering section, the great arc of plasma suddenly dissipating as *Dunstan's* particle accelerator drive went off-line.

Tumbling free of fast as light speed, the massive craft was thrown end over end into normal space and Fawkes could feel gravity's sweet attachment let loose moments before smashing face first into the thick glass of the observation window.

****

Fawkes had no idea how long he had been out before regaining consciousness. Opening his blood-encrusted eyes, he could see the stars had returned outside the observation window but they spun in quiet tiny circles.

Drifted along on momentum alone, its blackened nose turning over and over in one perpetual somersault, Dunstan was still alive but just barely.

Held firmly in place on the cold deck below the observation window, Fawkes could feel the artificial gravity had kicked in.

Rising up to his knees he looked about with his bleary vision; the control room around him a shambles, all flashing lights and gore. Blood coated everything, the flashing lights of the main console glittering like the deepest of crimson rubies.

Unsecured at impact, the cheerful if not slightly embarrassed replacement pilot had been thrown off his feet and through the control panel. His body had been severed in two by a collision with its shatter resistant glass, and pieces of the flight officer literally coated almost every reflective surface in the room .

Gaining his feet, Fawkes stood there in awed shock when a agonized, pitiful sound drew him back from the edge of absolute madness.

"Fawkesss...."

Deck had managed to grab hold of the command chair just as the electric wave sent *Dunstan* catapulting free of its course, but her arms and neck had become tangled in its safety straps. The way her body was twisted and malformed, Fawkes could only assume her neck and back had been snapped in multiple places.

"Fawkesssss...."

Masterson Fawkes stumbled through the wreckage towards her call, slipping in blood at the base of the chair and falling at her feet.

"It's gonna be okay, Deck. I promise," he pleaded with her, trying his best to get her broken body free of the snarl of twisted nylon without causing any more injuries.

Fawkes had no idea whether she couldn't feel anything from the neck down, and in her condition there was no way for her to let him know if he was causing more damage trying to help her... besides dying.

Finally free of the synthetic snarl of belts and straps, he laid her petite frame flat on the cold metal deck plates. Holding her head in his lap, staring down into her blood speckled eyes, Fawkes silently pleaded with her to jump up and save both our asses.

"Well, that was a fuck up of Titanic proportions," she spat the quip out from between lips slick with blood. Struggling to speak, drops of her life force dotted his face with the gentle touch of tiny butterflies on his skin.

"That's one way of putting it." Fawkes gently removed the blood matted hair from off of her face before asking, "Did you forget to push the Do Not Explode button?"

Deck's eyes darted about in her head, "Is comms down?"

“I have no idea,” Fawkes looked up at the gore coated console, its lights flickering beneath the meat.

“Are--” Deck stopped as her lungs tried to inflate, hacking hard as a fount of blood rushed up and through her lovely lips, “we still moving?”

“Yeah, but *Dunstan* is flipping end over end.”

“Did Michaels make it?” Fawkes could only assume she meant her replacement, silently shook his head no. Deck lay quiet for a second, her breathing shallow but her eyes quick with thought.

“We are lucky then...the EPod's backup generators and engines are online otherwise we would be bingo balls by now without artificial gravity.” Deck struggled to speak, every word quickening her death by seconds. Each syllable ripping open wounds hidden deep inside, filling her lungs with blood.

"Bad news is *Dunstan*'s dead or Captain Bonney would have already pulled us out of this somersault." Deck stared deep into Fawkes' eyes, trying desperately to convey the importance of her words with the strength of her gaze.

"Back up power is not infinite but that's not gonna matter. Eventually we are going to hit something or get drawn into the gravity well of a passing object and both are gonna' happen long before the power runs out.

"You've got to separate the EPod from *Dunstan*."

Staring down into Deck's blood spattered face, Fawkes could see the stone hard calculation flowing through her beautiful gold speckled eyes. Having trained all her life for this moment, knowing in the end it would cost her everything she had ever sworn to duty, Eleanor "Deck" Fillian was ready to sacrifice it all.

There were no words that could express the level of connection the two of them shared at that exact moment, she needed Masterson Fawkes more than anyone or anything had ever needed him in his life and he knew it.

Right now Deck needed him to save all of their lives and there was no way he was gonna let her down.

"What do I do?"

"Put me in the chair, my physical presence should start the back-up controls...."

"But moving you again could--" she could see the doubt momentarily returning to his face.

"Shhh..." Deck whispered, stopping his protests quickly. "Put my hand on the control pad to the right; it will bring up the emergency ejection protocol. Follow the instructions but use my hands to do it, flight control will only respond to the DNA of a command officer." Blood was flowing freely from her mouth now, as she choked to get out her last orders. Deck knew she didn't have much time left.

"Once you're free of *Dunstan*, wait for the EPod to achieve stability. The auto pilot and its booster rockets should correct the flight quickly after eject. Then go search the rest of the pod for survivors. There has to be a member of flight or engineering alive somewhere, they will at least know how get this bird to the ground somewhere."

Fawkes knew the moment he moved her body, Deck was going to die. The realization freezing him in place until she called out to him one last time,

"Let me die at the helm, Fawkes, please?"

Clasping his large calloused hands beneath her neck, Fawkes picked her up in his strong arms, cradling her like she had been his beloved for years. Deck's body shuddered as something in her frail frame give free, a warm deluge of dark blood soaking the front of Fawkes flight suit as he held her lolling, lifeless head to his shoulder and wept.

Lieutenant Eleanor "Deck" Fillian was gone, leaving Masterson Fawkes alone in a sea of chaos and madness, the only hope for over a thousand souls.

Gently placing her body in the command chair, Fawkes took Deck's right hand and placed it palm down on the control pad. A holographic screen instantly appeared above the gore encrusted console, flashing red with emergency warnings.

Using her delicate fingers, he set the pod for autopilot and eject. Klaxon alarms cry out and flashing red lights erupt all over EPod One, the computer quickly starting the 30 second countdown to ejection.

Holding on as tight as he could to Deck and the control chair, Fawkes felt EPod One shudder. The explosive bolts holding her to the main fuselage of *Dunstan* blowing us free before the booster rockets pushed us hard away from the tumbling mammoth.

It only took seconds for EPod One to right herself. As she gained stability, Fawkes could see the true damage sustained by *Dunstan*'s as her goliath nose passed within yards of EPod One's bow.

Most of the starboard section of the upper fuselage had melted away, leaving the interior compartments on the first seven decks open to the cold vacuum of space.

The charred remains of the bridge empty, dark, and dead. Captain Bonney was gone.

Dunstan's crew was on their own.

Midway back along her spine, sporadic fires twinkled behind thick observation windows running the length of *Dunstan*'s superstructure. The fear of being trapped behind those pressure sealed doors must be unimaginable. There would be no respite for the slow or confused.

When her underside came into view it was clear EPod Two and Three were a complete loss, giant ragged holes torn through their composite shell like a scar.

Four still seemed intact but was still bolted into the belly of a dying beast. Fawkes could only hope that their flight crews were scrambling to free the survivors from their inevitable fate.

Blindingly bright, *Dunstan* suddenly lit up. Blinking madly like some macabre Christmas ornament, it continued its cartwheel into oblivion.

The enormous amount of electricity *Dunstan* had absorbed in the plasma strike must have forced her reactors to scram the moment they were hit and now, as she danced across the night sky; with no one but the dead at her helm, a malfunction on board must have kicked the wrecked particle accelerator back online.

Dunstan was trying once more to jump between the layers of the universe.

The lights of the compromised titanium traps surged several times more before Fawkes watched *Dunstan* disappeared altogether. The only trace of her existence was a cloud of titanium bits and poly-nanocarbon chunks floating silently in space around EPod One.

Standing there slack-jawed, Fawkes momentarily thought about being stranded so far from Earth as shock and resignation tried desperately to take over. It only took a glimpse of Deck's broken body sitting vigil in her chair to add steel to his spine and muffle his pain.

Fawkes wandered off the flight deck, following the red blinking lights of the hallway out in search of survivors. Fawkes wandered through a war zone of walking wounded, mass congregating in the corridors with no particular place to go.

Everyone wanted to know what had happened. Wanting to tell somebody else about their terror. Wanting to know they were really still alive.

The ship seemed to be in one piece, but making my way through the common area was walking into hell, the dead and wounded littering the great hall. The joyous revelry of being the first humans to jump the great chasm of space had been replaced by pain and confusion.

Finding a flight engineer holding a bar towel to an open gash on his forehead, but still conscious, Fawkes yanked him up out of his seat, "You need to get to the bridge, there have been casualties to the flight crew!"

A clear look of confusion crossed the youthful flight officer's face as his concussed brain tried to focus on Fawkes face. He was undeniably impaired but inside duty overtook the pain. Years of training kicking in, conquering the fear, the flight officer headed quickly towards the bridge.

Med teams quickly made their way through the chaos, giving first aid and helping the truly injured down to medical.

After all the terror and excitement, Fawkes suddenly found himself impotent in the face of recovery. Security quickly moved in, helping the med teams return people to their quarters and without even realizing it Fawkes headed slowly back to the bridge.

Coming through the open doors, he could see the wounded flight crew member and several of the engineering crew were already working furiously to bring up all essential flight systems.

Big brother *Dunstan* had disappeared long before any of them ever made it to the bridge.

And yet the diligent crew soldiered on, trying to ignore the fact that they were all alone somewhere in the unknown universe beyond the Rim.

Continuing to stand guard at the helm though life had left her behind sat Deck. Death had called a hero home, and someone had been conscientious enough to try and give some dignity to her ultimate sacrifice by covering her body with a silvery emergency blanket.

Staring at the silvery silhouette of his tiny lover, Fawkes wondered if he would live long enough to think of her fondly in his old age.

Would the survivors of EPod One someday reminisce about how her sacrifice being the key to their continued existence?

Deck had done what any good command officer was supposed to do. She had given her last breath to save command and crew.

It was the least any of us could do, despite all this chaos, was mourn for her, he thought.

"You really shouldn't be in here if you don't need to be, sir." Fawkes heard an apprehensive security officer say behind him.

Pulling the blanket down and staring at the peace upon her face he managed to croak out, "She was a close friend, fellas. We had known each other for years..."

It didn't feel like a lie.

The flight officer who Fawkes first sent to help said something to the security officer, getting him to back off for a second. Leaning in he put his hand on Fawkes shoulder and softly stated, “We are going to need to get access to that command chair, sir.”

“It’s not a problem,” Fawkes whispered. He was so close to Deck now he could still smell that flowery perfume of hers mixed with up the coppery blood clinging to her rapidly cooling flesh.

Gingerly lifting Deck's lithe frame, Fawkes carried her away from this last command. Looking down on her in his arms, he couldn't see the blood or the pain anymore, all that remained was the beauty in her face.

As Fawkes walked away, the young flight officer sat down and started studying the holo-screen, desperately trying to figure out exactly what to do next.

Walking down through long echoing corridors, filled with the cries and sobbing of those too frightened to face the outside of their compartments. Fawkes didn't care.

No one knew what fate had in store for any of them. He had saved their lives and had nothing left to give the hidden and fear-stricken.

Finally finding Deck's quarters, her name painted in military text on a plate next to the door. Using her index finger to open the cabin door, Fawkes walked in to gently to lay her down on the empty bunk.

As the lights came up slowly, he found myself surrounded by a garden of delicate flowers. In oils and chalk, scans, photo paper, and holo-images; the walls of her quarters were a virtual cornucopia of activity and life.

The flight crew had been stationed on board *Dunstan* for over a month before the rest of the crew arrived and Deck had obviously taken that time to create a kaleidoscope of colors and images on the barren metallic walls.

Her quarters would have been a pleasant respite from the four year long, dark and empty trek across the stars at lightspeed.

Carefully laying Deck down in her bunk, Fawkes collapsed next to her on the floor. Despite the creeping shock and exhaustion, he stayed only a moment. Just long enough to gently brushed the hair from her forehead, close her beautiful eyes.

Rising from his knees, Masterson Fawkes kissed those cold lifeless lips once last time, leaving Deck to rest amongst her flowers.

Most
Beautiful
Moment
Ever

Most Beautiful Moment Ever

Wheezing like an old man and missing on two cylinders, Sally Jo Gustuvson's ancient Olds 88 screamed for relief but she wasn't listening.

This late season blizzard had come up out of nowhere; roads that had been clear this morning had become like boxing blind in phone booth. The thick fluffy snow pushed along by sixty mile an hour westerly winds hid a veritable minefield of crosstown traffic as she slung her old beater from lane to lane.

Sally couldn't think about anything but getting to the hospital.

The family had known for months this was coming. Everything they could have done to prepare for the inevitable had been done, exhausting every member of the family in the process.

Cancer was an evil bitch.

Her grandfather, Jasper "Pops" Gustuvson was as hard as North Range iron and had stood in the face of the inevitable for as long as could have been expected. He had suffered in hospice care for over a year. Even the angelic nurses who cared for him everyday were inspired by the tenacious grip to which he clung to life.

Pops had never done anything easy. Why should his death be any different?

He had worked the land for more than fifty years after coming back from the Marines and the big war. Pops didn't have any idea what the word quit meant. Even when the soil didn't want to give up anything but dust to all those around him, he made it feed his kids and keep the bankers at bay.

Her Daddy said it was all those years in the South Pacific with the Marines. *Jungle fight'n Japs in the dark. Crawling over volcanic glass to kill another man will change a person...*

Daddy had his own war stories from Vietnam and he told her once that each man has to carry the pain of war in his own way. If Pops wanted her to know anymore about it he would have to share it with her.

To his credit, what ever had made Pops hard, that strength had solidified his reputation as a true son of the soil.

Pops was a man everyone knew would be there when the cards were down and other men would give up.

When all was thought lost, that was when Pops' belly full of fire burned its hottest.

Back in ‘65 when Sally was barely three years old, when the Blue Earth River rose up outta' her banks and did her best to swallow the farm whole.

And Pops stood his ground.

Single-handedly Pops fought the waters back from his doorstep, what with Daddy off in Vietnam.

Digging in deep, mud up to his knees, slinging sandbags like he had no other purpose in life, Pops fought that damn river until it gave up and surrendered the homestead to him.

He worked night and day to put his world back into place, the fire burning in his eyes matching the one in his belly. When he got like that, Pop's was a machine, his intensity frightening to everyone around him. The family knew well enough to stay out of his way until he was finished.

He put everything into that farm, sacrificing every last piece of himself to make it run while raising his family.

The farm was gone now... After moving Pops to the VA hospital in the Twin Cities, Daddy and Auntie Rose made the difficult decision to sell off the land and the homestead.

Without Pops' strong hand, the old place just didn't have a heart anymore and the family neither wanted nor could handle the responsibilities. They all knew it was just a matter of time before the Blue Earth would rise up from its banks again and without its guardian where would the family be? Better to make a copper off it now than waiting for the raging waters of spring to take it all.

Pops wouldn't have ever allowed it but that didn't matter anymore, did it?

He would never know. The family decided he didn't need to know everything anymore. The stress was just too much for him in his fragile condition. Everything he had worked his whole life for was gone; except for his kids and granddaughter, and his body wasn't even cold yet.

No, they would never tell him. Even if Pops were coherent enough to understand, not one of them wanted to add more pain to his misery.

Cancer had torn down a giant of a man. Rusting the iron from his soul, his body paying the price for surviving. Little remained of the man Sally loved as a child, her memories filled with late-night campfires and early morning sunrises, summers of adventure and winters filled with hard work at Pops' knee.

In her mind he stood alone, out in his beloved fields watching as the burnt embers of sunrise rose on the horizon. Surrounded by an ocean of winter wheat, gently caressed by the lightest touch of early morning sun, Pops' rough edges of stone made flesh suddenly seemed soft enough to sweep Sally off her feet for a kiss.

It was a memory as beautiful as any painting. And that was all that was left now, a memory.

The rough edges had taken over, his flesh leathery and pale, taunt skin stretched so tight it barely covered the bone and sinew beneath.

What cancer could not take was the fire in his eyes. An angry, vengeful fire that seemed to carry on despite his mind's need for reprieve from the pain.

The VA Hospital in Minneapolis was shiny and new, less than a decade old. All in all, four stories of the best medical facilities in the Midwest and a bit of a maze for someone in a complete panic. Sally wandered about, lost in its institutionally bland corridors for almost ten minutes before finding her way to grandfather's room in the ICU.

Room after room, she found stagnantly sterile cells filled with broken soldiers like Pops. The age on their faces and injuries varied but the look in their eyes were always the same. Echoing black holes with knowledge of a great, terrifying secret they could never share with anyone.

It was only on the very verge of tears did Sally finally find her way with some help from a sullen young man with bright blue eyes, a shining smile, but only one arm.

The government ended up picking up the bill for all of Pops' medical care, which kinda surprised Momma and Daddy. The family had expected to go broke taking care of Pops in his final years. When Sally asked one of the hospice workers from the VA about it she said, "It was the least they could do for one of America's Atomic soldiers."

The answer didn't make any sense to the family but there were many things about Pops past he never talked about. What was important was it saved Daddy and Momma from bankruptcy, so there were no further inquiries as to the "why".

Standing in the door way, Sally looked down on Momma; worn and tired but still trying desperately to look her best in the face of the inevitable.

Who knew how many hours she had slept since they had moved Pops to the ICU? Sitting in a chair, her head gently resting beneath her father's withered but protective hand, Aunt Rosie was a mirror image of momma.

They both had done their level best to stay strong but the pain in their heart's hung on their faces like a mask; a grimace of despair replacing the images of joy Sally had known her whole life.

It only took a moment for momma to notice Sally lingering at the door, summoning up the strength to paint up a gentle, pained smile for her daughter's sake. Taking Sally by the hand and giving her a quick squeeze, Momma held a fingers to her lips while nodding to Auntie and Pops before leading her back out into the hall.

"Has there been any change?" Sally asked.

"He has been very quiet the last couple of hours but the doctors say he could go at any moment. Something about the stress from coughing was too much for his heart...he's been pretty doped up the last twelve hours to reduce the pain."

Sally could see the worry in her mother's eyes, the end had finally come, and after all this time preparing for it, Momma had no idea how to face it. “It's like he don't wanna live no more....”

Momma could barely hold back her tears and sobs, holding Sally so close she could feel her mother's heartbeat flutter wildly. Sally kissed Momma gently on her forehead before walking back into Pops' room.

The room was almost claustrophobic, filled as it were with blinking, beeping machines and stinking of industrial disinfectant.

Propped up in his hospital bed, Pops' dessicated body reigned over it all. His fragile frame like some grim master of ceremonies in the center ring, his struggling heart and failing lungs conducting the macbre' mechanized medical cacophony of a circus surrounding him.

the neckline of his gown stained brown with dried blood that seeped out from between pursed lips clenched together in excruciating pain despite the huge amounts of narcotics meant to make these last moments go by peaceably. The sight of it all made Sally want to cry.

There was almost nothing left of the Old Spice-smelling, honest-dealing, mid-western farmer. Sally fought back the tears at his bedside. His had been a hard life, the last thing Pops would want to see is her crying for him.

Sally couldn't know how right she was.

*

Jasper "Pops" Gustuvson fought his whole damn life for everything he wanted. This battle was one he knew he couldn't win, not that he wanted to win it.

Some people are just born to fight and Pops had it in spades.

His life had been one protracted battle after another. A literal war of attrition to survive and overcome a life filled with lingering hard lessons. It was a difficult path Pops had walked, each painful moment in time frozen in his mind like the icebound bloodied hands of his childhood.

Pops had never known his father. The man was a shambling memory devoid of any real life, his face lost to time. The only thing he managed to do in his short uneventful life was get killed in the Crosby mine collapse of 1924.

Officially the worst mining disaster in Minnesota history, the Crosby tunnel collapse and flood stole away many a father, brother, and husband. From Pops it took away any chance for a normal childhood.

His mother, heartbroken and suffering from long-term hysteria, took the tiny amount of settlement money the company offered. Family lent a helping hand, moving the two of them to her cousin's tiny dairy farm down near Rochester, where he just blended in amongst the seven other girls and boys while his mother just faded away.

What the land would give they took, working from sunrise to sunset, every member of the family pitched in to make it every day. Each of the eight mouths around their table knew they only got fed if every one of them made it happen. There was no other way.

In the winter it was the hardest, when the land had nothing easy left to take, but they made do. He and his cousins would work their frozen hands into a bloody mess harvest ice on the lakes and ponds for fifteen cents an hour instead of going to school or playing hockey.

When the war came Pops was barely seventeen. Compared to the bone grinding poverty of living on the farm, joining the Marines seemed like an adventure just waiting to happen.

Pops finally summoned up the courage to tell mother of his intention to sign up on a blistering cold morning in February of '42. Filled with patriotic pride and a desperation for change that only the young can truly appreciate, he pleaded with her to let him go.

She didn't even blink an eye, the expression on her face never changing as she sipped at her bitter cup of coffee. Mother had given up years before, not spending more that a few hours of the day outside of her room or to go to church.

She got up from their beat up table, put her blue flowered coffee cup in the sink. With a blank look of resignation, mother went upstairs, put on her best dress and drove Pops into Minneapolis to sign him up that morning.

Standing in the office of Colonel William Harding at the Marine Recruiting center downtown, this was the last time Pops saw her. She signed the papers to let Pops have a life of his own choosing instead of one that was forced on him by circumstance, kissed him on his cheek, and left Pops in the sure hands of the Corps.

Polio would take her home before he made it back from the war. Pops got the letter about her passing during the battle for the bloody isle of Peleliu. By that point in the war, his mind could comprehend the true depth of his loss of her passing.

Being hunter & hunted from Guadalcanal to Peleliu added a steel to his resolute survival instinct but it had dulled out his ability to care about the normalities of life. Surviving disease and the elements that took down so many others, Pops eagerly threw himself into the gears of industrial war time after time. His heart neared bursting as he ground up both man and earth alike...

Pops would never deny the kind of man he had became nor would he apologize. He was hard. The foundations for his life was laid in uncrackable ice but the South Pacific had reinforced it with volcanic glass.

His beloved Jesse knew it. She helped Pops to connect with a world that just didn't seem real anymore.

That quirky red head with an infectious laugh, her gentle touch like a moment of respite in a storm of shadowy memories. She had made it possible to come home from the Corps after the war. Jesse had saved him from himself, giving light to the darkness that followed him.

It was her convictions that convinced him to use his GI Bill to buy up the old farm and the property around back from the bank after his cousins lost it during the war. It was her smile that got him through the decades of frozen fields of winter wheat and swollen river water up to his crotch.

He had had built his house on the love of that perky little Red Wing woman.

When she passed away ten years back from the cancer herself, he had been ready to go then. After all that he had been through hadn't he earned the right to die?

Hadn't he?

Pops' body refused to quit on him, no matter how hard he prayed for it to end. Even now, near catatonic and on the very precipice of death, he found the strength to opened his eyes. The vision of his granddaughter stood before him, and despite the blurry vision she was still the living embodiment of his beloved Jesse.

It was only then Jasper "Pops" Gustuvson suddenly knew why it wouldn't end. Feeling it well up from somewhere deep inside, a single precious moment came to life right there before his eyes. As if struck by lightning, a familiar energy coursed through Pops' body and he knew the time had come.

**

Terrifyingly quick, the spasm suddenly rocked Pops' skeletal frame. His scarred and tumorous lungs fighting to expand, struggling for a single precious gasp of oxygen.

Sally closed her eyes squeamishly as a hypoxic seizure rocked Pops thin body. The poor old man's spasming arms shook erratically, the attached IVs and wires making him look like some a sad, possessed marionette.

Eventually Pops' lungs managed to relax, finding some hidden path through cancer-ravaged lungs, filling them with what little oxygen that could make it past the rising blood in his throat. As the spasms receded, Auntie grabbed a wet washrag to quickly wipe away the great gory mess from his lips but his eyes, almost animalistic in their gaze, paid her no mind.

They were trained intensely on Sally, frightening her to her core.

Rising up from his mattress with a strength no one even knew he still retained, Pops pushed hard at Aunt Rosie while reached out for Sally Jo with his skeletal fingers. The motion, almost like clawing at the air, was was gruesome to say the least but she knew this was still her grandfather.

Sally was his only grandchild, and he had shown her a side of himself that not even his children knew. His love for her was undeniable and there was nothing to fear from this poor dying soul. Just the thought caused a hidden embarrassment to well up like heat beneath her delicately pale skin, flushing it almost pink beneath her scarlet tresses.

Just as quickly as it had overtaken her, the cold, irrational fear that held her in place cracked like thin spring ice. Dropped her purse to the linoleum floor, Sally rushing over to Pops' side and took his frigid, hard hand in hers.

Pushing his flesh to her cheek, Sally hoped he could feel the warmth of life seep though his dry skin; her wet tears now flowing freely down her face. With the smallest, almost imperceptible of movements, Pops' rough fingers gently moved their way up and down her young cheek, trying to brush free her tears. She did not know this was a moment of approaching joy and this was the only acknowledgement of her pain that his body would allow while as he tried to summon and capture the energy within him one last time.

With the violence of what seemed like another seizure, Pops' frail frame came to life again, his feeble hands pulling his granddaughter's gaze up to his face. Staring deep into her eyes, Pops fumbled around beneath the neck of his flimsy hospital gown until Sally could hear a snap.

From beneath the soiled cloth, he pulled out a pair of beaten and weathered metal dog tags attached by an ancient broken leather cord. Dangling them between his wraith-like fingers, Pops grasped Sally's wrists and forced the tags into her hands.

Drawing her close; so near she could almost taste the copper-tainted, rot of death on his forced breath, he began to press her palms together so hard the steel tags cut into her skin. Hissed out to her from between glentched lips; speckling Sally's pretty panicked face with the blood of his dying breath, Pops asked, “D-o yyo-u want...to-o-o see-e-e the...mo-st be-auti-fu-u-l moment....e-ver?”

The metal tags in her grasp suddenly began to burn but Sally could break her gaze with Pops to see if the flesh was indeed rolling free of her hands. His eyes had begun to shine, bright like the fires that had forged the universe.

Once free of his skull the light crept and grew around them with octopodeian grace. Spreading like wildfire, the energy quickly engulfed the entire hospital room. Her mother, Auntie Rosie, the doctors, and all their blinking, beeping machines, they all just melted away into mass of expanding liquid fire rapidly escaping from Jasper “Pops” Gustuvson's shining skull.

Sally involuntarily closed her eyes as the primordial instinct to avoid blindness overcame her shock and surprise. The moment her eyelids shut, everything suddenly lost its depth; not able to feel anything but the heat between her palms. An eerie silence filled her mind as all sound in the room had disappeared as well.

It was as if the blinding energy that had escaped from Pops had swallowed all of reality. Sally felt light, like drifting amongst the stars as she floating aimlessly in space.

She had become one with the universe in one blink of her eyes and mere moments later, her mouth was filled with sand and blood.

***

"Gustuvson!!! Get your head down!"

Sally opened her eyes just as a pair of large of hands grabbed her from behind and thrusting he by the shoulders down into a roughly hewed dirt trench. The momentary disorientation of her fiery journey added to the momentum of this unexpected shove left Sally completely unprepared for the fall, planting her face squarely against the earthen wall.

The impact of her nose was immediate and sickening, as blood unexpectedly rushed into her mouth and down her face with an audible crunch

"MEDIC!!!" A blurry hulk in a green uniform hovered over the scared, injured young woman. "What the hell is wrong with you, Gunny?"

Her face throbbed in blinding pain and her eyes were filled with tears. Clutching at her face she couldn't see the face yelling at her from above.

“You drag my ass all over every fucking island in the South Pacific, talkin' shit about getting us back to the States in one piece, and now you want to stick your face in a fuckin' forge?” Slapping Sally on top of helmet she just realized she was wearing, the anonymous soldier continued to dress her down. “Put your goggles on and get your god damn head down, marine! Over here, medic!”

English was definitely coming out of his mouth, but it might as well have been Japanese because nothing escaping his lips made even one ounce of sense to Sally. All she understood was put your goggles on and get your head down.

Turned her back to the earthen wall, she pulled the thick ski-goggles down off her helmet and down over her eyes. The pain involved as the goggles came to a rest on the shattered bone and cartilage of her nose was immediate.

Blinded by the excruciating injury, Sally clawed at her face to yank them off until a gentle pair of hands came out of the darkness to her rescue. Pulling out on them just enough to relieve the pressure but not pull them off a mercifully sympathetic voice gave her a whispered, *Hush*, in her ear; making her feel she was ten years old again.

It was already late in the evening, stars bright in the night sky but with the goggles lowered it was like being back in the drifting void again. Her only contact with outside world these soothing hands and the chattering voices of the radio in the corner.

"Roger that Roman One. Diamondback two-four is in place. Diamondback two-four is in position. Light this bitch Roman One..." crackled out of the radio just seconds before a gigantic voice echoed out from pole-mounted speakers erected across the test site.

*"**H-MINUS: TEN SECONDS...***

NINE...EIGHT...SEVEN...

SIX...FIVE...FOUR...

***THREE...TWO...ONE....**"*

The ground rumbled with the sound of far-off thunder mixed with the sound of a sizzling hot pan of bacon fat. Sally's ears clogged as a thick, solid thump suddenly hit everyone like a sack of potatoes. The air pressure inside their dirt trench sucked out around them, replaced by hot gritty air that bit at her lips and exposed cheeks. The gentle angel that been holding on to her goggle was suddenly sitting in Sally's lap holding on for dear life. The pain in her face was almost unbearable and then, for just a moment, it relented.

For just a few seconds, even with extra dark blue-filtered goggles on, Sally could see everything around her bathed in an unearthly purple daylight. Rising out of the desert like a great man-made volcano, an atomic blast stretched up, towered over their trench. Its blast dome climbing to touch the stars as a thirty kiloton finger of fire plunged down to scar the earth with its purple fury.

Around the main pillar, raining down from the dome, tiny tendrils of smoke crawled down from the sky. The last of the purple fire inside its atomic heart swirling, climbing, trying to desperately to find more matter to consume withing its fiery forge; fighting for breath in the last moments of its life.

Fear and adrenaline mixed in Sally's blood like a two stage rocket as a cloud of microscopic glittering glass and sand assailed Sally's gentle face. She wanted to stand, rip off those heavy goggles and look upon this miracle of science with her own eyes.

She wanted to make love to it, run in fear from it, strip naked and bathe in its unforgiving glow until she looked down at the terrified creature curled up in her laps still holding on dearly to the front of her uniform. The unmistakable outline of her grandmothers face, lit up in the purple glow of atomic wonderment, stared back at her.

Slowly this man made sun disappeared and darkness took back the night sky. As the last shadows fell of her grandmother's face, Sally felt the weight from her lap dissipate, leaving her once more to float in the void.

She tried to pull the goggles from her face only to find just her flushed, dry, gritty skin. Reaching out into space for her grandmother, Sally felt a tear bite at her raw cheeks with the realization that she was gone.

****

Jasper “Pops” Gustuvson heart crashed moments after reaching out for his granddaughter.

Sally awoke laying next to his finally quiet and restive frame, cradled from beyond the grave by a grandfather that so loved her, he spent his last breath to pull her close.

As Sally opened her eyes, blurry in the bright florescent light of the hospice suite, her face was still feeling chapped and burned. Looking up at Pops' finally peaceful, almost gentle profile, Sally kissed his rough hands and whispered softly to him,

"You were right, Pops...

Most beautiful moment ever."

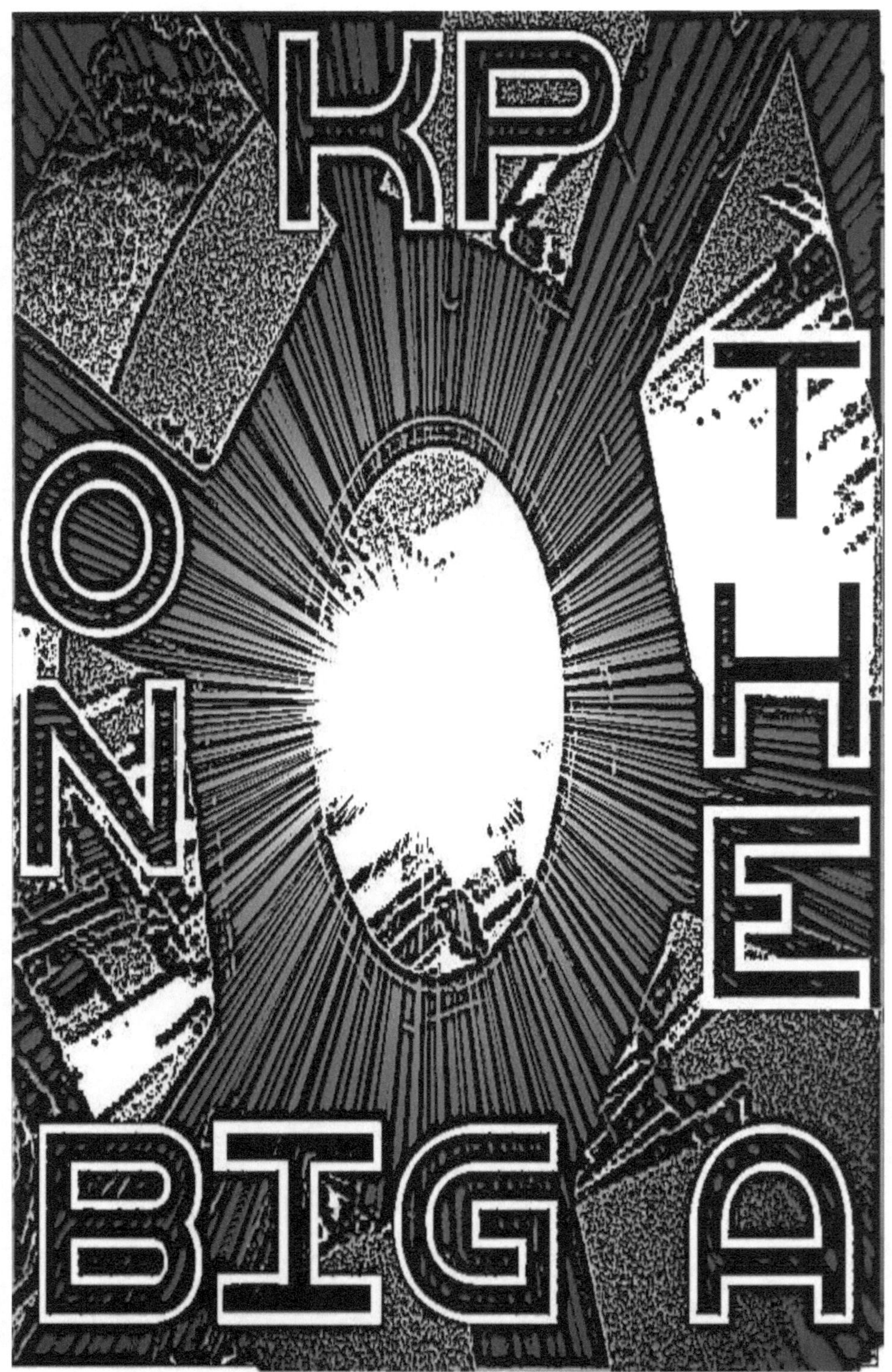
KP
ON
THE
BIG A

KP On The Big A

Silence will make a man go mad.

But it has to be a certain type of silence.

Most humans will never know what a true void of sound feels like until their final moment. The end of existence as the last synapses in the brain fire and the human part of us die..

That peaceful calm in the middle of the night snuggled in bed, this is not silence. The heartbeat of a city outside the window. Your husband or wife softly breathing beside you. The hum of electronics throughout your home.

There are a million tiny things that help create the peace one feels in those rare moments of "silence."

A true void of sound envelopes all, sucking away all vestiges of time and sensation. It leaves the brain behind to scramble about inside the skull, desperate to replace the comforts of the human soul.

The first week in flight school they teach everyone about aural madness, going over in great detail those dreaded moment when everything goes wrong. No expense was spared in their training. After the first week you should know how to stay alive long enough to make it to the survival pods and what to do once there to survive in its protective cocoon.

Lee Abner could hear the staccato voice of his drill instructor swirl all around him, the sounds projecting out of his mind and into the darkness with a life of its own.

“If you pay attention in this class, you will survive long enough for the angels of Search and Rescue to fish you out of the Big Black.” his lyrically terrifying tone screaming out, “If you don't, you will be dead and this class VI Apollo survival pod will be the box you are buried in!”

Frozen in place, the cold crept through Lee's arms and legs felt like they were being strangled by icy ivy, killing any feeling left in his extremities. Curled up like a child in its mother's womb, staring out of his fishbowl at the stars wondering which would come first, madness or death.

Memories were the only thing Lee had left in a world that had come completely apart at the seams.

*

Lee Abner reached that point of what to do when the music stops and the party ends at twenty years old.

He had tried to do what his parents wanted for him. Signing up for University. Attending what felt like a life-time of mind numbing lectures. Struggling through a stack of exams like any good kid should.

The problem Lee had with university was it felt like falling into a deep pool with no idea where the sides were.... and he couldn't take it anymore.

Yes, the old man had jumped through some huge hoops to get his only son into University but it wasn't as if he hadn't been waiting to do that for 18 years.

"No son of mine is gonna be tunnel rat," he used to say, reminding Lee every day of his life that he didn't want his boy working the mines was one of very few vices the old soy farmer from Minnesota allowed himself.

Unfortunately for dear old dad, Lee Abner was a re-alist.

In his mind, there was never any question where he was gonna end up. Everybody worked for one of the big boys. It was just a matter of whether you were gonna be clean or dirty when you came home from work every day.

More than ninety percent of his buddies went to work for EnerCorp or Agri-Nation; some heading west to the rare earth mines of the Southwest U.S. or China while others stayed close to home in the great agra-belt of the Midwest.

Most, if given a choice, would take their abilities off-world; the financial bonuses involved were just too lucrative.

With the void finally opening up her bounty to man and dreams of unlimited resources in outer space coming to fruition, a new age out in the stars had been born. If you had a skill, there was a market for it out in the Big Black,

Unemployment hovered at less than one percent since the off-world boom as the labor pool needed to reap the harvest of minerals and gas from the great asteroid fields of Kuiper's Belt was immense. There was no reason to go hungry when the partnership between private corporations and government was there to make sure you succeeded; whether you wanted to or not.

And with University out of the picture, Lee needed a job.

It was best to face the future head on, that was what his father had always taught him. “Never be anything but first in line. You don't want to see what happens if you wait for someone to ask for volunteers, boy.”

So on the last week of the semester, without letting his parents know, Lee Abner went ahead and scheduled his Career Aptitude Test (C.A.T.) at the employment placement bureau on campus.

The Bureau of Employment services was dreary little government-sanctioned office whose mint green walls hadn't been painted in his life time. A single bored secretary sat ensconced behind a frosted glass partition, telling him through a ancient crackling speaker to wait patiently for his turn.

Lee stare at the clock on the wall, every passing second filling him with nervous tension. What would he tell his parents? What could he tell them?

I'm sorry. Book learnin' was way too hard pops, I'm gonna go protect the universe...

Relief from his own mind came quick enough as a lanky man with balding hair and big plastic name tag that read “Employment Counselor” came out calling out in a nasally voice, “Lee Abner?”

The two of them wandered back through the maze of halls, ending up in a smaller, dingy room with a bank of old computers lining the walls. More than a few of the seats were taken so and the gangly bureaucrat gestured to the few open spots and left the young man to figure out his fate.

Above the testing areas was a curling and cracked propaganda holo-posters, each dingy and scratched but still active after decades in service. Designed to put a heroic face on signing away twenty years of your life, a confident dark-skinned man smiled down on Lee as “A life of luxury in exchange for twenty years! Heliah One colonization guaranteed!” flashed in fat red script above him.

Other posters depicted heroic space marines saving miners from burning transports out on the rim, nurses tending to the sick and wounded as engineers helping to create beautifully delicate new structures in the dangerous conditions off-world.

But it was the image of that man, sipping a cold beer and dipping his tanned toes in the warm sand of a holo-sheet paradise, that kept drawing Lee's attention from the endless series of questions on his screen.

That grin spoke volumes about the level of his happiness and it gave Lee the impression that for the first time in his life, he was making the right decision completely on his own.

**

“Boot” was a mind-numbing, body-pounding six weeks of safety training and phys-ed before each candidate was shipped off to their training assignments before final placement.

Lee had come through with few problems; he was still young and hadn't beaten his body with living yet.

After all the sweat and commitment of Boot, Lee dreams of heroism out on the rim grew exponentially. They say the training process made better men and women, so he was sure redemption was within his grasp.

Serving in the Interstellar Marines Corps or with the Marshal Service as a Lawdog were both admirable careers. Lee hoped his choice to defend the Rim would soothe some of the hurt feelings he had left behind in his rapid departure from the Twin Cities. There couldn't have been a more dejected rookie in Boot then Lee when he opened his C.A.T. Orders at graduation and was informed of his new life as a cook in the Commercial Naval Space Service.

It wasn't a bad gig. There were far worse jobs out there but Lee was still disappointed by the assignment.

Gone were the fantasies of heroism and adventure.... Hello minestrone soup and mountains of potatoes!

Having never touched a pot or pan in his life and no experience with the large industrial kitchens used to feed whole colonies, Lee had no idea what to expect but he was a realist. He would make the best of it.

When you went into the Naval Culinary Services, instead of the traditional four weeks of intensive classes in your skill set before permanent assignment, your first assignment was your training class. The training class was one whole tour long. One tour on the Atlantica.

Atlantica was a great shadowy shark of a spacecraft, the first and only vessel of her kind.

Sleek in lines with the heart of a dragon, the Big A carried a full five squadrons of attack fighters and rescue craft as well as an armament of five turret-mounted mag-lev-powered Mark 10 anti-matter guns.

Add in an unholy assortment of Class12 Tomahawk and Class 84 Harpoon spacial missile batteries, and this was one lady you did not want to mess with in the dark, she was fierce.

Above and beyond all else, Atlantica was the law.

She was Earth's hand in the void and there was nothing planet-side or out among the stars that stood a chance against her.

That's not to say she hadn't had to clear her voice in the twenty years since her commissioning. With her combat fighters constantly on patrol, guarding against smuggling or enforcing company regulations in the Big Black, Atlantica was always the center of action in one way or another.

Each of her pilots a government-sanctioned lawdog as well as an officer on the Big A, it took everything they had to keep the peace in a reality where lives were worth only as much as the time left on their contracts.

The only real scrape Atlantica really ever found her self in was during the great shipping embargo of '39. The result of long runs, thin profit margins and unsafe shipping conditions, independent freighter captains to call for a general strike out on the rim.

Naturally the strike spread like wildfire among the dirt farmers, as the hard labor of sonic mining out in the cold confines of Kuiper's belt compared with their meager contracts, left many of them with a sour taste in their mouths .

If there was one thing Enercorp would not abide, that is a stop in production; so Atlantica was sent in to toss some cold water on the squabbling dogs and help bring a swift end to what could easily turn into a negative profit situation.

It was the equivalent of calling in the S.W.A.T. team to settle a family squabble and a massive mistake. Cruising into EN 4653 Distribution airspace on the inner edge of the Kuiper Belt, Atlantica effectively shut down the window of ingress and egress to the five different refinery colonies by commandeering traffic control the moment she came in range.

More than a few independents, still not willing to carry their contracted loads, bristled at being held hostage till the strike had been negotiated and ended. There were other runs that could be made. Less profitable for sure but infinitely safer than the conflagration they had unknowingly started out on the rim.

Shortly after coming to and the first stand down orders hit the shortwave and broadband, four completely of the fully loaded small freighters along with a super-freighter: easily matching the Big A's massive girth tried to bolt from port.

Each captain hoping to catch the gun crews dozing and escape before Atlantica Command in control could completely set up combat air patrols.

In that instant, life on the Big A went from a humdrum boring day to controlled madness.

As the general quarters sounded ship wide, Command fired off a full complement of Atlantica's E.M.P. tipped Mark 10 rounds.

It was only meant as a warning shot.

The super-freighter captain, ordered to stand down by flight control, opened up all ahead full with his engines. Betting Atlantica's gunners couldn't come up with a firing solution before the his forty year old freighter's massive nuclear pulse engines could push them up and over the bow of Big A.

It was a loser bet and a mistake that would solidify Atlantica's reputation forever.

Programmed to pass harmlessly over the super-freighter, the firing solution was laid out so the five mag-lev-accelerated EMP rounds would explode for effect right over her bow. The pulse rounds, designed to temporarily shutting down the electrical systems on board the marauding mountain of a vessel, rifled down Atlantica's mag-lev tubes on course.

Unfortunately, the gun crews hadn't calculated for the captain's erratic maneuver.

The rounds tore easily through the multiple hulls of the massive super-freighter amidships, detonating in her cavernous cargo holds. The cascading series of explosions from the conflagration of millions of metric tons in hazardous materials on board the fully loaded vessel sent a tsunami-like pressure wave of metal in all directions.

In the moments before the concussion wave reached Atlantica, her bridge was deathly quiet. Every officer on board watched in cold horror as the vessel disintegrated, the magnitude of their mistake leaving the hardened sailors in shock.

What could have been easily worked out with a dozen marshals ended with two of the seven distribution stations knocked out of their orbits, all five of the independent vessels destroyed and nearly two thousand lives lost. EnerCorp payed out billions in settlement credits and Atlantica was stuck refitting in space-dock for three months over Mars Dome.

But the question of who ruled over the Big Black couldn't have been clearer.

Atlantica was the law.

***

On a warship like the Big A, one would think that the social order of the crew would be dominated by the gung ho types but Lee learned quickly after deployment that nothing could have been further from reality.

Napoleon was right when he said that an army marches on its belly, and a cook on Atlantica was well aware of the pros and cons of his or her position. The best bunks, high pay, and bonuses galore for multiple tours; an assignment on this battle wagon was the ultimate jump off point for a culinary professional in the Commercial Space Service.

She was also a mean evil bitch who would drop you where you stood on the line. The stress eating away your heart and soul til there was nothing left if you didn't have the steel to handle it.

With twelve thousand crew members serving on board the floating fortress, there are always four to five thousand active crew members who needed their three meals apiece. It is the solemn duty of the two thousand members of Atlantica's galley crew to make that happen without fail.

The pressure involved in feeding four thousand people is unreal at first.

Hours could fly by in a billowing aromatic cloud of sweat and sizzling hot steel. A whole battalion of highly trained cooks whirling around each other, actions in time like the workings of an ancient clock. Everyone who stepped up to the galley line and placed an order got exactly what they asked for, no exceptions. It took Lee almost three months to get used to the routine, to find his rhythm.

At the end of his first tour, the old timers congratulating him with massive bottles of Rum and Serenity station pussy for making it out to the rim and back in one piece. In the midst of the mind numbing debauchery the old hands warned wilth fuel smelling breath, "Getting into the rhythm is the easy part, boy. You gotta pull more than five tours before the weirds set in. Survive the weirds, and you can call yourself an ol' hand."

The weirds...

A condition found almost exclusively among the galley crews of Atlantica and the deep-space mining operations out on the belt, the weirds were a mystery wrapped up in a nightmare. Characterized as "psychotic outbreaks with little or no reaction to outside stimuli", none of the headshrinkers from Earth to the Rim could diagnose a cause for the weirds.

Was it the long hours? The stress? The lack of connection to a stable family life? Who knows? But once exposed to someone in the throws of a weird outbreak, one can never forget it and always remembers to pray you never get it. Lee got a full taste of it on his third tour.

Two weeks before making Ceres station, rumors started to circulate 'round the galley concerning one of the old timers on B crew. Atlantica, like any close-knit, tight quarters community, was not a home for secrets or privacy.

One couldn't take a funky shit on board without somebody else knowing about it.

Slipping on his apron that fateful morning, Lee searched the assignment board only to find Master Chief; the head chef and master of the galley crew, had decided to pull him from his normal station on meats to help out on fryers. A change of assignment wasn't unusual, Atlantica had no shortage of loll-abouts and drag-assers.

It wasn't until he saw who he was scheduled to partner with did Lee get nervous.

Word was Stuckie, an ol' hand with more than ten tours under his belt, was showing signs of the weirds. Repeating conversations, taking chances on the job, reckless behavior on R&R; Master Chief had seen it before and had scheduled for Stuckie to get a medical transfer once they reached dock at Ceres Station.

Until then, the Chief had decided to stick him with a babysitter, and that was Lee, figuring the young, stable cook on his third tour could help keep everyone safe on fryers till Ceres.

The first rush came and went pretty easily, thousands of faces flying by in a blur of fresh food. Michael “Stuckie” Stuck; a tall, balding fellow from Alaska, pushed through the breakfast service like a muscular machine.

All smiles and wise cracks, Stuckie and Lee pushed out a metric tonne of bacon, eggs, and hash browns in their first four hours. Food flew off the hot tops and out of the fryers with precision, filling the bellies of four thousand crew members just starting their shift.

Having met Stuckie during their last furlough at Serenity Station, Lee didn't notice anything strange immediately. He seemed to be that same jovial, bear-like man who liked to get twisted on Canadian whiskey and throw away stacks of credit on any poker table he could find.

Not once in those first four hours did he ever come off as crazy.

Midway through the second rush Lee noticed a shift in the vibe. Still coherent and jovial, Stuckie was keeping up with the workload but had gotten really quiet.

He never missed a single order, but had stopped communicating; the silence throwing Lee off his game and causing the brigade to falter just a bit.

Lee knew plenty of other people that got that way; especially midway through the day. So he just put it out of his mind and kept pulling boxes of frozen shrimp, fries, tater-tots, and chicken for the bubbling maul of the industrial sized fryers.

Stuckie didn't snap until halfway through the dinner rush.

Lee had just come back from the freezers with another box of frozen potato skins when he noticed Stuckie almost hypnotized by the mesmerizing bubbles floating on a sea of golden brown oil in the industrial sized hot fryers.

Without warning, the moose of a man just bent over at the waist, plunging his head and arms below the surface of scalding liquid without hesitation.

There was no screaming, or none that escaped his lips. Just the squeal of boiling oil as it mixed with water from Stuckie's frying flesh filled the air.

Despite what must have been excruciating pain, Stuckie climbed further into the massive fryer bank, turning it into a volcano of boiling fluid, spilling its contents out on the galley deck while trying its best to cook him whole.

Dropping the spuds to the deck, Lee pulled the plugs from the wall and rushed to his partner's aid.

With the fryer's power gone, its super-heated vegetable oil started to cool immediately but that didn't stop the scalding liquid from attacking Lee's flesh with molten fury.

Despite the excruciating pain he grasped firmly to Stuckie's spasmodically twitching legs, trying to free the dying man from his self-imposed hell.

In the end it took three hard jerks to yank Stuckie from the rapidly congealing prison, the crazed man's hands continuing to clutch at the coils deep in the bottom of scalding liquid.

Even with all his strength, Lee couldn't find the leverage to to pull Stuckie out until the man's thick fingers burning through from holding on to the laser conductive heating elements for so long.

All at once, they both came free, collapsing in a greasy pile on the deck as Lee screamed, "Medic! Medic!!" His piercing cry drowning out the cacophony of a mess hall in full stride.

There was nothing recognizable about Chef Michael "Stuckie" Stuck. With the hair and loose flesh burned free of his torso and head, a crispy mass of raw flesh and nerves melted into the shape of a man all that was left.

The entire galley crew stopped and stared down the half-mile-long line; not knowing what to do as Lee sat there and cried for his lost friend.

The weirds had claimed another victim in Atlantica's gritty, grease encrusted galley and the last moments of Stuckie's life were as permanent entrenched in Lee's mind as the scars on his forearms.

****

It was so cold.

Struggling to keep his eyes open, Lee didn't have the energy to do anything but lie there. The only sensation left to him was the last rumblings of Atlantica vibrating through deck and into his frozen flesh.

Lying there in the shadows, all he could do was to wait mercifully for sleep.

Lee silently hoped it ended this way. To die in the gentle embrace of oxygen deprived sleep and not the clawing clutches of the Big Black just outside his window.

Those were his last wishes.

*****

The end of a tour is an exciting, chaotic time for Atlantica. While the crews of engineers and grease monkeys at Serenity Station go about breaking down and cleaning up the Big A during her yearly maintenance inspection, the thousands of men and women who make up her crew abandon the captivity of Atlantica's cramped quarters for the exotic smells and sounds of Serenity's bazaar.

It's petulant pleasures far away from the pressure, stress and confinement, this was what the crew worked for all year. Business owners on Serenity station both celebrated and dreaded Atlantica's arrival, knowing the approaching storm and accompanying chaos as well.

There were profits to be found in the pockets of rowdy sailors out for a good time and EnerCorp was always prompt in paying for anything they broke.

A month is a long time to be out of rotation on the big battle-wagon, regardless of your duty assignment. Four weeks of furlough gives one the time to think. Time to reconsider. Time to cut a new deal. That's why Serenity Station was your first and last stop of any tour of the Big A.

Fresh blood flowed in from the C.A.T. stations, old hands bled off to new assignments or retirement. This was the cycle of life on Atlantica.

Not that thoughts of a different life had crossed Lee Abner's mind.

Stepping through her airlocks, Lee could hardly believe this was his tenth tour, Atlantica's familiar smell of oiled metal and recycled air welcoming him home. As a newly minted Master Chief, fresh and in charge of a brigade, Lee had put enough good time in on the Big A to write his own ticket anywhere in the system. and had gotten a deluge of messages during his vacation about transferring off the Big A.

Offers had come in from as far way as Earth and the Keiper One mega-refinery. Each one bonus sweetened, with contract extensions marked time sensitive; their terms only valid during Atlantica's downtime at Serenity Station.

No one would have faulted him for asking out.

Lee was an old hand, having spent his entire adult life in the furnace of this floating fortress. He had become a man in her guts.

She had left her scars on him and kept him safe from the deep cold outside her portholes. The only thing about him that remained unchanged after a decade with her out amongst the stars, Lee Abner was still a realist.

With ten years left on his contract, all a transfer would get him was a change in venues and more years.

Yes, he could be planet-side. Serving fine food to corporate execs on their lunch break in luxury under Mars Dome but it would still be the same job. And the expense, my lord, the expense!

It would take every credit he earned just to afford a place to live.

Lee had gotten used to life on the battle-wagon. Atlantica was like living in a bank vault. Uniforms, food, entertainment, a comfortable cabin, all part of the deal.

Some men literally spent a king’s ransom in credits during their furlough on Serenity Station just because they had it to spend. Lee was never one of them.

He was a realist, keeping his expenses at a minimum while still having a great time. He didn't need satin sheets when cotton would do.

Another couple of years and then Lee would think about a transfer but not now.

Let the credits stack up a little higher and then bust out of the Naval Service in style was how he figured it. Maybe buy his way out of the rest of his contract and open a small place under the Dome.

The great thing about being a chef, there is always people who needed to eat.

******

Four months on Atlantica can fly by once you get back behind the line. There were some missing faces but enough familiar ones to make it seem as if nothing had changed.

Time disappears as the repetitive nature of life on the Big A kicks in. Even after the twelve hour days start to take their toll, it's still business as usual. Days blend into weeks and the weeks just melt away.

Occasionally a holiday will come up or group of rookies fresh to the belt would be forced to eat a whole plateful of "asteroid"-sized meatballs upon our arrival at the rim. These were just momentary distractions from the monotony to an "Old" hand.

The only real difference for Lee on this tour, besides the promotion and extra duties, was a good bunk assignment. Apparently with rank and seniority come rewards because cabin with a view and only one roommate was like being royalty.

On days when life became overwhelming, and his mind wandered to dark places like Stuckie and his fricasseed face, Lee could stare out at the Big Black to release all the tension, irritation, and pain built up inside his soul. Over the last four months Lee had gained a true appreciation for the beauty of its ever changing canvas.

With his bunkmate was on the opposite shift, Lee barely knew the guy.

He seemed like a nice enough fella, real bad at poker but neat, polite, and private... all the things one wants in a good roomie.

But it was the twelve hours of peace and quiet from being on opposing work schedules that Lee really appreciated.

Masturbation on board a deep-space craft like Atlantica followed the same rules as actual sex: you take it where you can get it and hope you get the most out of the short time you got.

Lucky for Lee, having just woken up, was still lying in his boxers and t-shirt so there wasn't much in the way of getting the deed done.

Prepared to make the most of his time alone, Lee pulled on his boxers before he notice the light blue glow of Neptune softly illuminated the darkened cabin. Distracting him from his moment of self-gratification, Lee climbed free of the bunk and stood before his observation window, bathed in the magnificence of a giant.

Lee had witnessed Neptune's cerulean beauty before but it was always in passing. Standing before his porthole, he realized the view from a dingy utility bay windows had never done it justice. It was so personal this time as she crept into view, its rippling wind-tossed atmosphere a celestial pool, filling the iris-shaped window like a magnificent azure eye.

As Atlantica maneuvered closer in to a safe orbit, the industrialization of Neptune became readily apparent. Giant spider-like refineries and their docking facilities, a towering mass of storage tanks and glittering lights gently hanging in geo-stationary orbit over the planet's equator.

Figuring out years ago that radiation issues on Neptune Station would always keep profit margins slim, EnerCorp kept the human presence to a minimum. Rotations at Neptunian Control Center were kept short, the refinery rats kept around just to keep the bots up and running. Ninety-eight percent of the actual work force here was robotic.

With just fifty-five men to run all eight of the gargantuan facilities at Neptune Station, every man was essential. If the human control teams were disabled somehow, it was an immense and immediate problem.

With no eyes to watch the multiple reactor cooling levels, or hands to correct the occasional robots off station, disaster was inevitable.

As Atlantica's captain delicately sidled the great battle-wagon up to the docking facilities, alarms rang through out the Big A. Vessel-wide word went out that rescue operations were about to begin, her medical crews prepped to proceed just inside the airlock doors.

Watching the docking clamps reach out for Atlantica's great frame, Lee's mind started to wander, thinking about pantry inventories and requisition forms. With the addition of new souls on board, even terribly sick ones, the numbers would have to be set right. He be damned if he were the first Master Chief in Atlantica history to run short of anything in the galley's history.

The explosion was perplexingly fast and stupefying in its intensity, Lee was caught unaware as the nuclear reactor powering H processing plant two exploded. Exposing their core and ejecting tons of red hot radioactive material and steam all over the the insides of refinery, the conflagration once started was unstoppable.

Torrent of destruction consumed anything flammable, which was pretty much everything, and fired it out directly into Atlantica midships. Neptune Station's transport hub acting like a cold steel cannon, funneling the forcefully escaping molten gases and debris into the Big A like an improvised dirty bomb.

Thrown across the room by the concussive blast, Lee was knocked unconscious as hit the deck as hurling huge chunks of radioactive refinery tore through Atlantica's thick skin. Her great sleek superstructure collapsed in on itself amidships, turning the Big A into a twisted mass of shrieking destruction.

Klaxons all over the vessel went off while red lights pulsated along the floor and ceiling. Magnetically-sealed cabin doors released with a clank and hiss, receding up into the walls automatically. Abandon ship protocol called for all personnel to follow the red lights to one of the many banks of survival pods on every level of Atlantica. From the deck, Lee shook his head, trying to clear the cloud of concussion out of his skull as the alarms and blinking lights relentlessly filled the air.

From where he lay, Lee could see through the cloudy red haze that his door had raised only four inches.

The door frame of his cabin had crumpled as the shock wave rippled through Atlantica, and there was no way it was opening any further. Scrambling across the deck on his hands and knees, Lee tried desperately to shove himself beneath the frozen door.

Steel edges cut and scraped his skin but that didn't matter. He could neither feel the pain in his panic nor free the frozen slab of metal; the bent metal keeping the door locked firmly in place despite his efforts.

Stretching out, Lee was barely able to get his arms out beneath the door past his elbows. Screaming like a madman for help as hundreds of feet, booted and bare, ran just beyond his grasp. The alarms and collapsing spacecraft clamoring for relief easily drowning out his voice in the madness.

Not one person noticed the flailing arms struggling to escape.

Pulling his arms back under the door, Lee lay on the floor, heart trying to beat free of his chest. As the claus-trophobic reality of being trapped started to set in he sprang for the floor and rushed over to his porthole, hop-ing he could identify how bad the damage was from his perch.

The chaos outside the foot thick quartz glass was undeniable. A virtual scrap yard hung between him and the bright blue face of Neptune. Massive scorched and glowing bits of refinery mixed in with Atlantica's remains, almost completely obscuring the view of the majestic giant.

Mashing his face flat against the cold glass, Lee could see a quarter of the aft section of Atlantica float off towards the gravity field of the planet. Having been amputated in the broadside blast; the entire aft section from the Main Gun number three to her tail tumbled away, spilling her guts out to the stars.

As man and his machines were flung out into the frigid expanse of the Big Black, explosive decompression began to blow its way through Atlantica's remaining compartments like an invisible battering ram,

Sitting quietly back down on his bunk, staring blankly out at the chaos.

Lee Abner was going to die and he knew it.

****

It took two days for auxiliary power to fail, finally allowing Atlantica's corpse to go dark and cold. Lee's quarters, although lit by Neptune's gaze, was like a frozen meat-locker. The opulent azure glow making the chill worse, even if it was only in his head.

At some point in the long hours since the accident the remains of Atlantica had fallen into a stable orbit above the planet and stopped eating herself. Those compartments still sealed holding on tight, froze in place as the frigid touch of the Big Black caused her metal to contract and lock into place.

There were definitely survivors.

Over the last forty eight hours, Lee watched as a cloud of tiny survival pods shoot away from the hulk of Atlantica. He had stopped worrying about being rescued a long time ago. Lee Abner was a realist.

Once the power goes on a spacecraft so does the heat and life support. Anything still taking breath on board would freeze to death in hours.

No light, no heat, no oxygen... no chance for survival.

Hunger pains ripped at him but he was far to cold to move. Snuggled beneath his mattress, layered in as much clothing as he could wear, Lee was reminded of winters from his childhood. Of those frigid Minnesota mornings when no matter how many layers he put on, the biting cold would still make its way in to needle his frozen flesh.

Soon the hallucinations would come. His brain was drowning in a sea of carbon dioxide. Every shivering, stuttering breath slashing time off the clock of life.

But that didn't matter to Lee.

By that time, he was back already back home. Safe and warm in his grandmother's tiny kitchen back on the lake as she sang a sweet song meant to sooth away his fears.

Lee Abner would hold on to life for fifty-six hours in that little cabin.

Staring blankly at the big blue eye of Neptune, her gentle storms finally lulling him to rest and sleep in her arms.

****

Command Master Chief Lee Abner awoke in a warm pool of viscous blue liquid, and for a moment thought he had been swallowed whole by Neptune. One of only three hundred twenty-six survivors of the incident at Neptune Station, his frozen body was not recovered for almost three months. Trapped in the radiation safe confines of her hull, those who had survived, did so within the wreckage of Atlantica herself.

The Big A protecting them all to her very end as the official investigation would later note.

The majority of those shot away from the wreckage died in the first twelve hours from radiation poisioning. The rad protection on *Atlantica's* Class VI Apollo survival pods were rated for "normal" emergency space exposure, designed to keep its inhabitant alive for a week in normal space.

Not shielded for a full-on rad-bath from that big blue giant, the thousands of pods ejected away from the *Big A* became coffins. Each crew member perfectly preserved for burial in a gentle orbit around Neptune.

Freeze or fry. Survive or die.

These are the only choices one is given out on the rim.

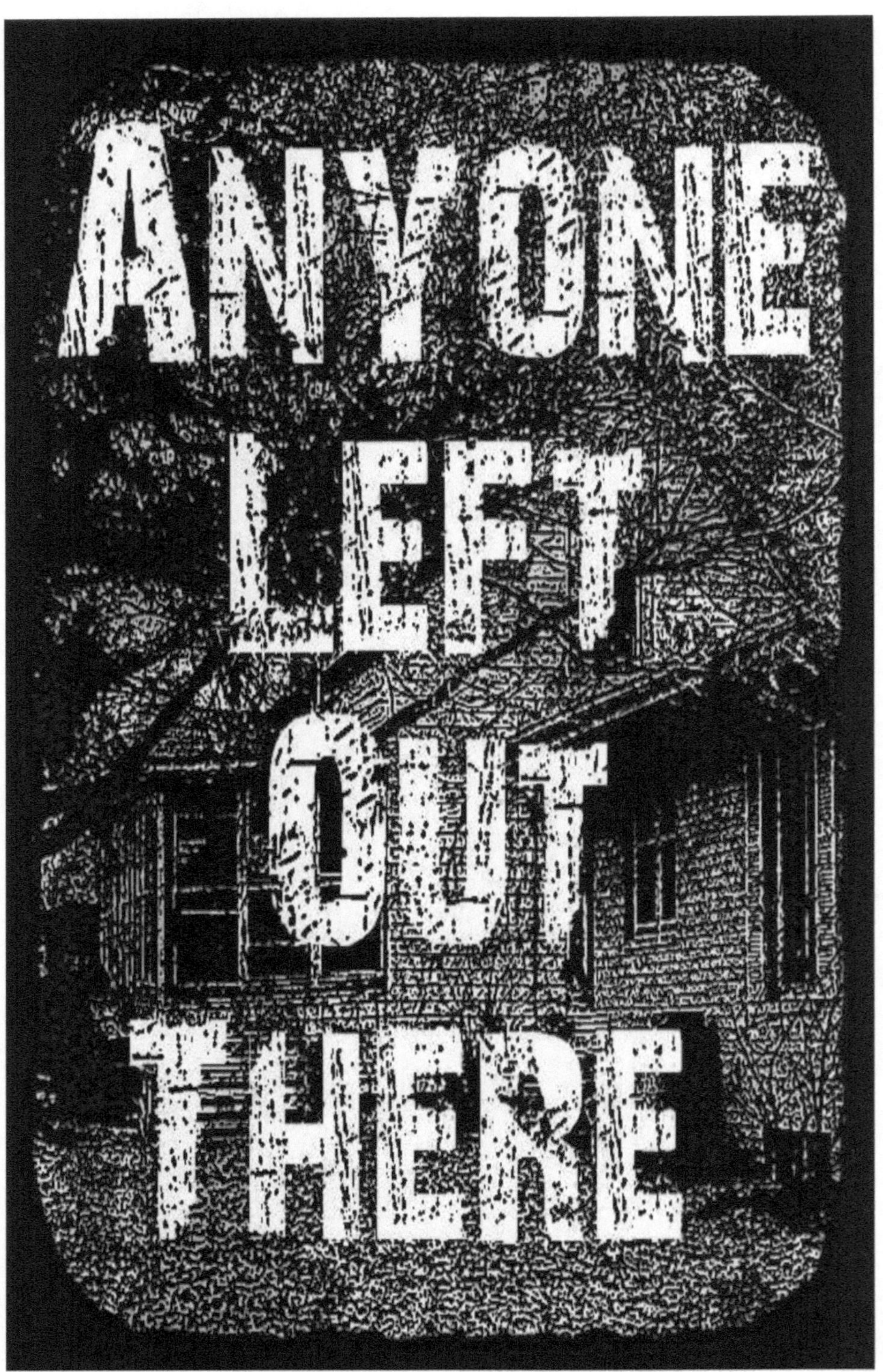
ANYONE
LEFT
OUT
THERE

Anyone Left Out There?

"I can't believe the system is still up and running....

"Don't get me wrong, I'm not hatin' on my geek brothers and sisters out there. Someone's technical Kung Fu is running on overtime to keep the virtual lines of communication open internationally because the local shit has been as dead as my neighbors for weeks now.

"I expected the satellites to continue to broadcast for awhile, even if the television landscape of the apocalypse is all reruns of reality TV shows filled with people that are long dead by now but I never expected the net to hang around as long as it has. Blowing my mind, man!

"You won't find much chat on the ordinary boards and chat rooms anymore but iReporters around the world were flooding sites like NPR, BBC, CNN, and Al Jazeera with all kinds of video reports.

"Kinda' got to the point where I was like, "Does it matter, man?" Everyplace looks the fuckin' same when the whole damn planet has been turned into a war zone.

"Yeah, I saw the pics of Russian tanks sitting abandoned in front of the burning Kremlin. It was like looking at hollow iron soldiers guarding over Red Square; a modern terracotta army of Xian. Empty, lifeless, waiting for time to bury them in snow and ash.

"Apparently the Vatican stands while Rome burns....I heard its private army of Swiss Guards are fighting to the last of their numbers to protect the holiest of sites in Europe from annihilation.

"Places like Zürich, Munich, Frankfurt, Florence, and Venice are eerily quiet, as if they don't exist anymore. I read a post by someone in London posted about massive gravitational anomalies all over Europe right before CERN labs in Switzerland went silent.

"Yeah, I heard the same rumors about nuclear explosions on the Korean Peninsula and along the Pakistan/India border but nothing hard or substantive as communication coming in from both areas is sparse at best. I guess even in the face of total annihilation, ending age-old religious and political scores were something familiar to cling to when compared with the alternative.

"China? Nada, man. That place is locked tighter than a drum. Nothing going in and nothing coming out.

"The last live television I saw? That was over a week ago....yeah, the meltdown at CNN Center in Atlanta.

"Man, that was hard to watch, like some Rodriguez-esque slaughterhouse film. I swear it was like watching that Road Warrior live on TV.

"CNN Center had been a Fortress of Solitude down in Atlanta before some rogue National Guard unit formed up for their last stand there. The last bastion of real information on the airwaves crumbled in front of HD cameras at the end of the world and it was not pretty.

"To be honest, the most disturbing part was afterwards, watching a cold, silent newsroom filled with the bodies of those we once trusted and loved lying in the wreckage; the cameras continuing to run long after the players had left the stage.

"Did you see it? I uploaded the last two hours of broadcasting last night...yeah, you can still get it via this link to a Brazilian server still running.

"On a similar note, the Cities has a Katrina vibe, brother.

"The skies over Minneapolis are way quiet. I watched for weeks as convoy after convoy of helicopters, lighting up MSP with traffic. Then about a week back: nothing.

Air traffic out of MSP has been all military for a long time now but even that has died off now. Yeah, it all suddenly just stopped. No planes, no trains, no automobiles and definitely no more Blackhawks.

"I guess the one percent was done packing up, having deciding to sit through the apocalypse out of town and I say fuck'em! Run and hold up in your man-made caves, assholes! Hide away till the country has stops burning then pick up the pieces...what a great plan.

"Humpty Dumpty, bitches....

"Civilian traffic? Nah, that has been non-existent since an incident three weeks back....

"Some asshole with a pilots license and a death wish commandeered a private plane with a group of survivors and took off without permission; I could see it all with my telescope as they taxied off and tried to make a run for it.

"Nah...they didn't make it very far. The remnants of that Lier tumbled out of the sky about eight blocks from my house.

"I figure they nailed it with some form of surface to-air missile because it rained fiery chunks of metal and the conflagration burned for days.

"The average person like you and me...well, bubba, it might not be ten feet of water but the cavalry ain't rushing in to save our skins any more than they did for those poor folks down in the Superdome.

"The world is going quiet in a burning pyre, brother. Each city twinkling out like stars in the sky as the last fires burned out and the dead rule over a kingdom of ash. There is no escaping, only hiding... waiting for the cities to become our mass grave.

"Sorry man, got a little poetic there. I'll try back in a couple of days and see if you're still hangin' in there."

*

"Have you been outside recently?

"Dude....I had to venture from my house today, hoping to find something edible. One doesn't shop for the apocalypse on a budget, man, so I am ill-prepared, brother.

“Having been cooped up inside so long, just the whisper of a fresh breeze on my face felt almost alien. Add that to the silence....I got so weirded out I ran back into the house and cowered in my living room for almost thirty minutes.

“No shit, man. The only thing that drove me back out the door was that gnawing pain in my gut reminding me that hunger trumps fear.

“There aren't many vehicles on the streets anymore but I left my car parked where it was. No sense getting it stuck or attracting attention, I might need it later, ya know?

“Besides, I only live a couple of block from one of those super stores, so I figured a quick hike over and back was the best plan. The hump would be good for me and I could get out quick and quiet if need be.

“You should have seen it as I approached, man.

"I lived through the L.A. Riots and Seattle during the WTO protests but have never seen anything so chaotic in person before. The sun high in the sky, doors laid wide open like a pumpkin the day after Halloween as looters like myself scrambled in and out of its dark mouth looking for one last scrap of anything to help satiate the hunger.

"Nah, it was like flies crawling on a bloated corpse. The other survivors didn't seem to even notice me unless I got a little to close and then it was just a warning glance, eyes filled with as much pain and fear as ferocity and violence.

"The front was a shambles, brother...

"Making my way to the warehouse in the back took forever as I weaved in and out of barren aisles full of crushed displays. Even in the dark it knocked me back a bit to see how quickly this store had been emptied out.

"I was in that place a month back and it had enough crap in there to feed a small country. Now it was a ghost town.

" Kinda glad I worked for one of those places before Barb and I moved to the Minnie in '06. It made navigating the dark, tight confines seem a little easier.

"Yeah, I know. Dumb-ass move; anything could have happened back in the dark, but I just knew there shit was back there.

" Every warehouse manager I ever met hated marking out damaged goods and always end up with a giant box back by the dock. I found a case of bottled water in the back along with a whole mess of dented cans in a bin obviously designated for damaged goods. Thank god for the mediocrity of small minded individuals, right?

" Shit yeah, I stuffed what I could in my pack, shouldered the case of water and started back towards the hacienda baby. I slid back in to the front of the store; quietly, ya know, and that's when all hell broke loose.

“ Hell no... I had no idea what all the fuss was about, but all I could see from behind a smashed jewelry counter was a small crowd that had formed around the bright sunlight marking the wide open entrance.

“I totally panicked man....huddling down in the broken glass and cheap jewelry as paranoia rushed into my veins like acid.

“I thought about all the bad shit that was about to happen to me. Had they noticed I wasn’t part of their raiding group? Were they gonna take my meager, beat up cans and week worth of water? Could I really fend off twelve real live people with my aluminum softball bat?

“ That moment right before you die, everybody talks like its some ethereal experience but I'm tellin' you man, it ain't filled with pictures of your life. Nah, man....it's just your brain frying as you try to scheme a way out of the inevitable.

“Fortunately for me, I didn't get a chance to linger on that shit for long. Why?

"You ever hear a Vulcan Mini-gun go off? Yeah, like the one *Jesse Ventura* carried in *Predator*.

"It hums baby... 'till the rounds get downrange which is exactly where I was. Then it's just explosions and terror, man; a hailstorm of shells cutting through the flesh, bone, metal, and glass like meat in a sausage grinder.

"To be honest, I just curled up in a ball and prayed for it to end because I couldn't think of anything else to do.

"It's the god damn end of the world and I'm gonna die 'cause some trigger happy mother fucker found a new toy and decided it would be awesome-sauce to test it out on some poor slobs that took their one chance to survive.

"Talk about fucked up karma....

"So, yeah, I'm lying there, pretty sure I'm wearing little chunks of people that used to be my neighbors; when I here this fucking amplified voice boom through the now deathly quiet store."

"ANYONE LEFT IN THE STORE NEEDS TO STEP OUT! IF YOU HIDE AND WE FIND YOU, YOU WILL BE SHOT. IF YOU SURRENDER PEACEABLY, YOU AT LEAST GET A CHANCE."

"Now, I might not be the smartest guy in the world, but being a hardcore gamer back when the world was normal, I learned a long time ago any statistical chance you have to survive is always better when the other option is definitely death. So I walked out.

"With my backpack and the case of water in my outstretched arms, I stumbled through the gore and slaughter at the front door and out into the bright daylight to face my fate, brother."

"PUT YOUR GEAR ON THE GROUND AND GET DOWN ON YOUR KNEES! YOU ARE UNDER ARREST FOR VIOLATING MARTIAL LAW AND HAVING BEEN CAUGHT IN THE ACT OF LOOTING; WHICH IS A COMPROMISE OF NATIONAL SECURITY. BY THE POWER GRANTED TO ME BY CONGRESS AND THE PRESIDENT OF THE UNITED STATES, GOVERNOR MARK DAYTON AND THE GREAT STATE OF MINNESOTA. IN THE NAME OF THE LAW, I HEREBY DECLARE YOU GUILTY OF THE CHARGES OF LOOTING LEVIED AGAINST YOU AND ORDER YOUR DEATH BY EXECUTION."

"No shit man, just like *Judge Dredd*....

"Six different heavily armed soldiers came down on me like white on rice, throwing me down into the muck, screaming unintelligible at me from beneath gas masks. It was the scariest moment of my life man and I will never fucking forget it.

"I think I even pissed myself a little when one of them put an AR-15 to the back of my head and pulled back the slide; chambering up the 5.56 mm round that would turn off my lights forever.

"I heard, "Does the guilty party have any last words?" this time without the megaphone and I just started gibbering man....straight running off at the mouth.

"I swear to God, I have no idea what I said to the man but something good must have come outta' my lips because the next thing I know they are helping me up off the ground and pulling off their masks to smile at me and my predicament.

"Word of advice, fella..." one of the guys shook out a smoke from a crumpled sweat stained pack of smokes, put it between his lips, and tossed me the rest. "The Cities are Bravo Delta you know? Total shit. Downtown is a slaughterhouse, and the capitol is split up into two factions, those that want to get out and the ones who want to try and help those that are left. Unfortunately, the ones who want to split run the show; so this place has got a real short shelf life if you get my meaning."

"So, I says to him, "Where in the Hell am I gonna go, man? There is no way for me to get into the capitol. Unless you guys need another set of hands?" I hoped and prayed they would say yes.

"Not a chance, man. We are en-route from Monticello to the Prairie Island Nuclear facility and got no time for stragglers. We gotta shut down the reactors in this area before there is no one left to do it."

"Yeah, imagine that. This bunch of assholes who had killed twenty or more people over dented cans of peaches and moldy toilet paper, were the same guys responsible for shutting down the nuke grid across the Midwest before half the northern hemisphere glows."

Stepping up, an older guy with six stripes up and down his chest epaulet looked me dead in the eye while slinging my back pack up on my shoulders and helping me get ready to move, "Listen up! There's no one patrolling the streets anymore; the ground is no man's land. Anybody staying behind needs to find their own way."

The grizzled old top sergeant pulled a 9 mm pistol from a clip-on holster and a couple of mags off his bullet-proof vest before slipping them into my backpack silently. "You live a couple of blocks from here?"

"Yup," I say.

"Grab that case of water, and stay frosty, kid. This is one hell of a soup sandwich and we all get a bite."

"I swear, dude, I turned and ran, never looking back."

**

"I actually thought about going into work today... isn't that strange?

"I woke up this morning in my comfy chair on the second floor, firmly locked away and hidden from the world. Enveloped by the warm red leather of my captain's chair, somehow I forgot where the hell I was.

"Looking around for the kids and wife, I just figured they had already left for school and she was already on the air as I stumbled into the bathroom to stripped bare in front of the mirror.

"No, I haven't any idea what I was thinking besides, "It is definitely getting cold again," as I reached into the shower curtain to turn on the faucet. It wasn't until I stepped into three foot of murky gray water I have been using to clean my clothes since the power went out did I snap out of my fugue and notice what I was doing.

“I swear that was the moment I finally realized there was nowhere to go.

“Crouching down in the frigid liquid and I cried for like twenty minutes.

“The kids are gone, Barb is gone; I am all alone and no one to blame for it but myself. I don't even know what happened to them. The last call was before the cell phones went down and that was over a month ago.

“Yeah, eventually I got dressed, perv.

“You know what I saw outside the house today? At first I thought it was snow but after sticking my hand out the window, nope... it was ash. I climbed up on the roof and you can see it creeping across the Cities far off to the north, towards downtown Minneapolis.

“There is no sunlight anymore. The smoldering remains of the Twin Cities has overwhelmed the glory of the sun with a greasy black ocean of smoke; the remains floating down on me with the gentlest touch of flakes of snow.

“How is the power supply in your area?

“Over the last twenty-four hours there have been rolling blackouts, and the smoke and ash accumulating in the atmosphere has completely disrupted the television signal and is making it hard to connect to the internet via satellite service..

“Yeah I know it doesn't matter. But even with the programming gone it was still reassuring to see a color bar, ya know? An illusion of reality to cling to....

“There is another terrible fire to the south, burning on the horizon like an impending sunrise. I just hope it has nothing to do with Prairie Island.

“Months have gone by. My potable water is gone, food has been scarce for far longer and I know this might seem strange but I’m kinda scared to be trapped in this house with the cat anymore.

“Zod has always been strange, but the look in her eyes recently is that of “Just die already so I can have a decent meal. I never had much hope, and that is really starting to wane.

“I guess the question one has to ask at a time like this is “Do I really want to survive anymore?”

....503 Service Unavailable....

“Fuck....”

THE RAYS
Commercial Naval Space Marshal Service
COMMERCIAL NAVAL SPACE SERVICE
MARSHAL
A DIVISION OF ENERCORP
HOUSTON, TEXAS
OF NIX

The Rats of Nix

Star Marshal Johnston Kipling coughed hard, trying to clear the stale bitter taste of scorched metal and deep space ice from the back of his throat. He knew what to expect from this derelict long before stepping through its frozen over airlocks.

In the past eighteen months the Interstellar Transportation Safety Bureau had been called out seven times for popsicles just like this one. Two weeks off the beacon, the ship was purposefully settled into a stable orbit, undamaged with the exception of where their airlock was popped.

Each vessel carefully powered down by the book with the command crew tucked neatly away in hibersleep pods. Life support left running on auxiliary power to protect its crew from the unrelenting cold found in the creeping void.

On a routine return run back from the Kuiper Belt, her payload bay full from one of the orbital refineries, the crew had settled in for the long trip home. Its Honeywell-built Inertial Measurement Unit (I.M.U.) locked on to the processing ring at Lunar One, hydrogen pulse inertial engines cycled up to full power.

Two or three days in, long before clearing the last traces of the debris fields on the belt, their entire ship was shut down as if by remote. Guidance, flight control, even the damn food processor units were shut down.... everything except life support.

Johnston had it figured after the third job, he just had to put the pieces together in the real world. See, keeping the command crew tucked away in their hibersleep pods was an integral part of their plan.

Not only did it keep pesky witnesses out of the way during the heist, it also kept the meticulous pirates from riding the lighting for an interstellar murder rap.

Once the vessel is floating dead in the black, it turns into just another strip job; anything of value that didn't endanger the lives of the crew is stripped clean. With nothing but gristle and bones left, the vessel is parked right off the beacon, waiting patiently in the cold and dark for someone to find it.

These bandits were clean, professional, and above all else efficient. They never gave any hint as to where or when they set up the heist, why they chose these particular ships, and left no real trail behind to track their egress.

There was no rhyme or reason behind their acts of piracy. Not even the mega-computers back in Houston could put together a pattern with predator association software. They were literally like ghosts in the corporate machine.

More like rats hiding in the bowels of an abandoned ship, Johnston thought to himself.

He respected these men. Johnston Kipling hadn't grown up wanting to be an Lawdog. Locked into a contract just like everyone else, the only real difference between him and these "privateers" was a badge.

Every crew Johnston helped to pull in surprised him; each filled with a plethora of different personalities and trade. Doctors, miners, ex-lawdogs, and scientists; it was never the same. The only thing they had in common was the desire to make a life for themselves outside the bonds of the corporations.

Everything changed after the loss of *Atlantica*.

Johnston had served two tours early in his career on board the Battle-wagon and a great many of his friends were active officer's on the Big A at the time of the disaster. More nights than not, sweat soaked his sheets while the imaginary terror of his unconscious mind trapped Johnston within the destruction wrought on her once-graceful, warlike lines.

Waking cold, the spartan space of his quarters little comfort from the endless metal halls and fiery hell of his nightmares. He would never be free of the memories.

Marshal Johnston wasn't alone. Not one person that crawled free of that wreck was the same and the same could be said for police presence in the belt. With *Atlantica* out of the picture, the long arm of the law was stretched to its limit as the new realities out on the rim settled into place.

Piracy was as old as humans navigating by the stars; from the first time man decided to move valuable things across the big unknown to make their fortunes on the other side, there have been other men dedicated to stealing it.

These post-*Atlantica* times were no different.

Hundreds of thousands of vessels traverse the gravity swells of the great solar seas every hour of every day and the bureaucracy involved with keeping millions of extra-terrestrial vehicles moving and doing their jobs safely was a colossal headache; even when things were working the way it is supposed to.

When you threw these brigands into the mix, it was just a matter of time before someone was going to die.

Marshal Johnston knew most days it wasn't required to run one of these groups to ground. Generally catching them red-handed in the act was the most expeditious way of dealing with pirates. Eventually, someone will make a mistake and that's when you scoop them all up in one net. Any little fish that got free would get picked up in another run somewhere close.

This new group had changed the game.

Their only perceivable weakness was their leader. He had a flair that showed in a very particular way, and that was the only reason Johnston wasted his time coming out to this frozen asshole in the middle of nowhere.

The medics were already on station, moving the crew onto a rescue craft for shipment back to the medical station at UB313 and defrosting. A replacement crew was inbound to transport what was left of the ship back to Jurisdictional Investigation Headquarters at Mars Dome.

With full pressurization restored and portable oxygen recyclers pumping fresh air into the vessel; Marshal Johnston Kipling moved down the open corridor towards the bridge, his boots clicking against the frozen metal deck plates like flint on steel. He could have waited the twelve hours until they got back into port but he had to know if his hunch was right before making the call.

Crossing through into the bridge, its pressure doors frozen open like like the gaping maw of a darkened cave, Johnston shook his head at the destruction. It would take a half an hour for the engineers to get the power back online to defrost this useless hulk and months for the techs back at Mars Dome to go through the mess.

All along the iced-over panels and displays, tiny blinking lights were starting to pop on; bathing the cramped control room in a shimmering sea of aquatic blues and warm pinks that rippled like water off the icy walls.

Pulling out his mini-mag flashlight, Johnston stalked straight over to Flight Control, and illuminating the crystallized bio-control panel with his torch. What he found there brought a small smile to his mustachioed lips.

Yup. A flair all his own....

*

Nix.

Back in the early days of deep space mining, it became obvious to the architects that autonomous floating refineries would be an ideal solution to the cost-prohibitive nature of trying to move billions of tons in unrefined precious ores and materials out of the belt to resource-starved Earth. But even those massive facilities would still need a main transport hub and originally that was Nix.

With a diameter of less than fifty miles, Nix was the middle child of satellites orbiting Pluto. In comparison to the rich pickings of the Kuiper Belt; Hydra, Nix, Charon, and P4 had no real redeeming value to the company when the system was going through its initial mining assessment, with one exception.

Nix's composite silicate core surrounded by a thick shell of ice may have been deemed a waste of resources as far as a mining operation but the architects envisioned a purpose for the strange elliptical shaped satellite.

In one of the greatest feats of modern inter-spacial construction, Nix was hollowed out and in place of its removed core, the main Plutonian transport hub was constructed.

A marvel of cutting edge technology, Nix Station was built strong enough to survive if there were a cataclysmic failure of the surface ice or the remainder of its silicate shell. Designed to float free as one gigantic survival pod, Nix would establish a geosynchronous orbit around Pluto on its own until help arrived to assess the damage.

However, because it was privately owned by EnerCorp, the ingenuity of its creation was quickly forgotten back in Houston as time passed and the active mining operations moved further away from Pluto's orbit.

The new inner belt hub, Neptune Station, was constructed in orbit just outside of the radiation heavy zones around the same time the massive mobile command platform *Atlantica* was commissioned into service.

Funding for the project eventually dried up as fewer and fewer profits came in, and Nix was declared cost in-effective.

But that is not the end of the tale for Nix.

It has been twenty-two years since EnerCorp decommissioned Nix, shutting down her reactors and sealing the doors. And yet there is still some life left in her.

**

"A book is a special thing. Within its pages is an arrangement of words that can make you laugh or weep. But did you know it holds an even greater secret within its cover? A book carries with it through time and space the very essence of life."

Kristos Lamont grinned widely as he juggled four leather-bound volumes in the low-grav air around his head, moving in and out of the thirty or forty people that had gathered, he danced in rhythm with his bouncing bobbing books.

With long languid movements, Kristos spun about and cleanly snatched one of the books from the air while continuing to deftly handle the two others in flight. Holding it open with two fingers, showing off an old copperplate ink sketch of a knight, he handed it down to a little girl sitting wide-eyed at his feet.

“There was time when to even look upon the printed page was a crime, oh tender youth. Yes, to dream is to dare, and with that you commit an offense against God as well as your betters, they used to say....”

Where there were once two, a third book had once again reappeared in the flying orbit above his head. Kristos gave it a strange look before capturing it as well.

Flipping the pages with his fingers to a sketch of monks earnestly working a printing press, he handed this one to young man trying desperately to not look interested meandering near the edge of the group.

"For a man or woman to find freedom, one first had to find the written page and for many a long year that was how man controlled other men.... By hiding the truth of the page," and all of the books floating around him suddenly disappeared entirely.

Peeking over his shoulders like paper bound birds, they hid from Kristos as he looked left, right, and between his wide-spread legs for the impetuous tales. Reappearing moments later, joined again by a third volume as they came up from behind his back, the dancing troubadour spun on the balls of his feet. Securing all three between his large hands with an audible slap, he trained his gaze on the crowd.

"Dreams are a fleeting thing in the face of hunger. Almost impossible to catch with your children starving in the muck, or a soldier's blade in your guts," opening his hands, the books flew from his fingers into the air high above the entranced audience.

Followed quickly by a stream of its brethren from a pack strapped to his back, the three volumes were now twenty or thirty, all dancing merrily above the head of the awestruck onlookers.

"While there are some that can caper on in the face of adversity with but a belly of blind faith; it wasn't until we had the freedom to learn, that man did 'stretch the surly bonds of earth.' Just by reading."

Slowly the books descended from their frenetic, fanciful celebration. Each finding a face in the crowd to belong to, causing a small smile to appear on even the hardest visage among them. "In that one act, we were given the ultimate gift. The right to truly live free from the yoke of other men.

"So, read! Read children and parent alike! Everything you learn is something *we* all learn! Everything *we* learn makes us stronger and it is in that strength that *we* as a community survive. A healthy mind is the key to surviving the Black!"

Bowing deeply in his billowy red shirt sleeves, leaving trails on the dusty deck as the back of his hand touched the warm metal. Bounding back upright as if his spine was made of rubber, Kristos flashed his wickedly best smile to the applause of the children who swarmed around him.

The crowd dispersed quickly, there were always things to do on Nix. The little urchins scrambled off to their homes, precious treasure tucked between skinny, gravity deprived arms as a few adults from the crowd came up to shake Kristos' hand and give him an ol' fashioned "Good show, Doc."

Nix was a hard place to survive.

Once a utilitarian space station designed for the care and maintenance of deep line vehicles, it was never meant to be a permanent home to anyone.

And yet here she was, worn and dirty but still bustling with life. Her nine cavernous hangers, each two miles deep and a mile wide, having become miniature cities to those with no other home in the universe.

After Enercorp abandoned Nix, the derelict space station promptly became the respite of smugglers and thieves. A perfect place for the exchange of pilfered and purloined non-corporate-sanctioned goods, it wasn't long before the first bedraggled shanty town went up to cater to the ragtag collection of cutthroats need for vice.

For nearly two decades of flotsam and jetsam had drawn in human refuse from all over the solar system to Nix. Hanger bays One through Seven became tiny towns with their own languages and customs, and Kristos knew them all.

Nix had become a haven in the dark, a living ghost town on the rim of the solar system.

When whispers started to circulate in the underbellies of long haul freighters and military command ships about a world outside the control of Earth and her corporations; they exploded like a ripple on the Big Black herself. Waves of information that would eventually make their way it back to Houston.

Yes, Enercorp knew about the squatters on Nix.

They just didn't care.

There wasn't any stop of profits and the takeover hadn't cost them anything. If there was ever a need to regain control of the station.... Well, there were plans in place for almost anything.

Doctor Kristos Lamont had made his way to Nix via the long haul, as some called it here. Life, having decided his world was too comfortable, gave him a shake up, causing him to start all over.

Once he had been a theoretical physicist and mechanical engineer, one of the legitimately great minds of the last century. Kristos' breakthroughs in designing the first anti-hydrogen envelope drives were supposed to change the whole universe, fueling the great migration into the dark beyond the rim with engines that could approach the FTL-Einstein barrier.

The only problem was they didn't work.

There was no way to stabilize the envelope completely. Even with the anti-hydrogen drives at seventy-five percent, the build-up charged particles between the envelope and space-frame could theoretically produce a plasma-like backlash that could severely damage or destroy any vehicle.

It was all theoretical, of course. Until it wasn't.

Kristos couldn't reproduce the effects in a lab or on the test ranges; not that he hadn't tried, and in the end Enercorp didn't listen to him.

The math never lies...

Those engines were going to fail.

Despite his objections and concerns, Enercorp put the engines into production for the Heliah Colonization Expedition. When contact was lost with the lead vessel Dunstan right after launch, the entire system wondered what could have struck them down but Kristos Lamont already knew.

Math never lies.

So he resigned his position at EnerCorp, slowly tried to put his life back into perspective but one reoccurring equation haunted him.... How does one make up for causing the deaths of five thousand people?

Kristos had no answers.

It was a math problem that had no solution.

So he bought an old ore transporter with the fifty percent retirement EnerCorp granted him and floated about the system, contemplating the problem on his whiteboard of life.

Time alone in the Big Black will change a man, even in the comfort of a vessel designed to carry a million metric tons of processed ore converted to a mobile one-person space station. *Versailles,* as he re-named her, home for all those long years when the slow time crawled by during his search for answers.

Kristos collected thousands of items, filling her holds with the refuse of a technological world. Books, maps, paintings; lost trinkets that used to be symbols for wealth and intellect on Earth discarded like refuse, were treasure once more in his cargo holds.

The longer he spent out in the black, the less likely it seemed an answer for his moral dilemma was likely to appear. As the math played out over and over again in his head, Doctor Kristos Lamont gave up altogether on any type of equitable solution.

That was why he shut down the lights and retired to his hibernation chamber for the long sleep. Hoping, if ever to wake again, time would clear the ledger. That was not to be.

In the darkness, long before time could claim him, Nix embraced his frozen animus and it was in them that Kristos found an answer to his sorrow. The collecting, bargaining, and smuggling; years spent filling his cargo bays with knowledge, it was all for a reason.

The baubles weren't to bring him joy in the midst of his guilt.... No, he was to be their conduit. This was his sacrifice and penance, a mountain of retirement credits spent to better their situation on Nix for just one moment.

His was to be the life of an intergalactic intellectual Hurdy Gurdy man, bringing knowledge to those who had saved his soul when it meant the least to him.

As time passed, Kristos began to dream of bigger plans for Nix, not content with just peddling his baubles and wares. Low-grav hydroponics bays would save these people from their strife, so quietly he began the process of trying to collect all the pieces and put them together.

Like Shelly's monster, the massive gardens that overwhelmed hanger bays eight and nine like a great rain forest, grew from the remnants of the dead but they were there. As luscious and green under the bright grow lights as the sun back home on Earth. Fresh food, oxygen producing trees, cash crops like tobacco and cannabis for the black markets; life had found a way in the Big Black.

But the maintenance; Lord, the maintenance! Kristos was always putting together lists of “must haves” items for the scrounging crews. No one ever questioned his mad manifests, he had done too much for the people of Nix for them to doubt his judgment now.

Why? They trusted him. The sincerity always rang true in his deep brown eyes and the firmness of his grip; Kristos never busted a deal nor abided by a deal-breaker.

As the gardens started to emerge, so did the communities around it.

No longer just living off the scraps some smuggler drug in off a supply vehicle or wreck, the forgotten on Nix could see the light of creation right in their midst. Passion exploded in their eyes when tasting delectably crisp celery between their lips or touching the bark of a growing sapling for the first time.

Some of these kids had never seen plants before, their entire lives having been lived on the inside of a dead moon far from the warmth of the sun, the little ones fascinated by these completely alien creatures that wanted nothing more from life than water and light in return for their bounty.

The gardens had become a point of pride to the lost souls of Nix. They finally had a purpose, and people with a purpose are extraordinary creatures. The only thing standing in the way of long term survival on Nix was power.

Water was never an issue. The entire surface of Nix was ice and the way recycling was routed on this bucket they would never run out. The problem recently was producing enough power to keep life support and basic utilities running.

The oasis growing in hanger bays Eight and Nine was a power hog, sucking everything they hooked up to the main power grid dry with its endless banks of water regulators and fluorescent grow lamps.

Built with alternate emergency generators, Kristos and Nix Council decided early things weren't dire enough at the time to light up Nix's multiple nuclear power-plants. It was best to leave her main power reactors cold and dormant to avoid run ins with EnerCorp.

The company might know the abandoned space station was "inhabited," but the council decided there was no point in pissing off the bull by waving a red flag in its face.

If they kicked on her reactors, Nix would burn like a bright light in a dark room. Her massive power signature, so far out on the rim, would advertise she was back in business and that would surely bring an army of unwanted attention.

Everyone on board realizing that very act would draw a cold calculated response from corporate in Houston. The last thing anyone wanted to see was a battalion of space Marshals come through those airlocks; black body armored shock troops intent on clearing out the riff-raft with whatever force they deemed necessary.

So Nix lay dark and Kristos drove himself to the edge of madness every night trying to figure out her puzzle. From theoretical to applied sciences, he had gone over every source of alternative energy in his head.

The answer was out there, he knew it but without those reactors off-line the math spoke for itself. A single major power outage would wipe out the fragile Eco-system Kristos had worked so hard to build. With the gardens gone, these communities that so eagerly worked together now, would turn on each other like rabid dogs with out hope.

When the last of the juice ran dry, a power struggle for resources would inevitably rage in Nix's narrow corridors and dirty shanty towns. Death would reign free in the chaos, and all of this would be gone; leaving Kristos once more back at the beginning with guilt in his mind and blood on his hands.

Packing up his gear, Kristos tried to put that dark thought out of his head as a hollow voice echoed out from the shadowy corners of the old command center, "The key to survival for any pirate haven is the apathy of the civilization off which it is living... magician."

Kristos froze; his right hand still inside the leather book satchel at his hip, it closed quietly on the concussion pistol among the tomes within. The voice was unrecognizable, with no hint of any of the many Nixian accents.

It was too clean, too precise, too Earth.

“So... what draws the attention of The Almighty Enercorp, lawdog?” Kristos turned, pistol raised, slowly training on the sound of the shadowy figure.

“Popsicles, magician. Or should I address you as Doctor Kristos Lamont?” Marshal Johnston Kipling stalked out of the dark, holding up his hands to show he wasn't armed.

Johnston had been among them for weeks, hidden in plain sight. Clad in a beat up mining uniform, and just as dirty as ninety percent of the rats living in this derelict. Johnston smuggled himself on to Nix in a shipment of nitrogen conversion fuel cells originally bound for Mars Dome.

It had taken a lot of effort to ingratiate himself with a ex-long-haul pilot turned "independent," but it was funny how the threat of six months in an Anechoic anti-grav cell will open doors that want to stay closed.

Once on board, Johnston was amazed by Nix. Expecting to be greeted by a rough and tumble outlaw camp, akin to the mining stations out in the belt: dirt on the floor, blood in the corners, and all manners of vice within the grasp of any man with the wares to trade or credits to transfer.

What he found instead was every bit as orderly and civilized as Lunar One or Mars Dome; real communities having sprung up in this far-flung remnant of a moon.

Twenty thousand souls called this relic home and despite a few truly undesirables walking about, Nix was a serene peaceful place.

All thanks to Doctor Lamont and his gardens.

Drawn to them like a moth to flame, watching night after night as the little children of Nix cavorted madly in the bright lights and misting spray, Johnston couldn't deny its beauty. They were pure genius, a patchwork of scavenged gear and inventive engineering, with thousands of hours in its design and construction.

The fact that the good Doctor had made this all happen right under the noses of the snoopsters back in Houston made the feat truly extraordinary.

“Well, you know my name... lawdog. Does this give one power over a man, knowing his name?” Kristos' hand trembled, shaking the big pistol while trying to keep it trained on the space Marshal.

He has no idea what to do with that piece of steel, Johnston thought.

Not wanting to spook the good doctor, the Marshal slowly took one of his empty hands and gently put it in his pocket.

Pulling out a bent and folded holosheet, he held it out to Kristos, "No, but figuring out their words and thoughts do."

Pulling up an old office chair, Johnston settled down while Kristos looked over the holo-sheet and lit up one of the hand-rolled cigarettes they sold here by the handfuls.

Tobacco was completely illegal back on Earth but there was always somebody trading it out on the rim. The Marshal's Service could never nail down where the supply of gaspers was coming from and now he knew why.

"Good product, this. But when you have a fresh supply growing by the acre, I guess it's not hard to put out a decent smoke, is it?" A cloud of gray smoke trailed from beneath his long red mustache.

"That ain't one of the originals mind you, those are safely back in my office at Mars Dome but I was just wondering how it sounds read by my voice compared to the one in your head," Johnston cleared his throat with a hard cough before easily reciting the words he had spent so much time looking at over the last year.

"We must be as stealthy as rats in the wainscoting of their society. It was easier in the old days, of course, and society had more rats when the rules were looser, just as old wooden buildings have more rats than concrete buildings. But there are rats in the building now as well. Now that society is all ferrocrete and stainless steel there are fewer gaps in the joints. It takes a very smart rat indeed to find these openings.

"Only a stainless steel rat can be at home in this environment."

Kristos tried to not show his hand but the Marshal's perfect impromptu recitation left him secretly smiling on the inside.

"The Stainless Steel Rat" was his trademark tag for sure. Harry Harrison's adventures fueled his idealistic youth with dreams of adventure out amongst the stars.

It was a work he treasured above all else, and enjoyed reading the tales of *Slippery Jim DiGriz.* The scavengers whose jobs it was to find the bits and pieces that kept Nix turning out in the Big Blacksaw the grifter as a hero which is why he had made a few holo-copies for some of them.

But how or why this lawdog had a copy and traced it back to him was a complete mystery to Kristos.

Putting on his best poker face, Kristos tried to play it off, "I'm sure the Master Harry Harrison, would be delighted to know after all these years that his work is so widely known. To be honest, I always thought the "rat's" voice was suaver, with more of a Latin lilt to it."

"And I thought you would be taller," Johnston quipped. "We seem to be having a polite little conversation here, so why don't you holster that heater so we can discuss what's really going on?"

Kristos carefully slid the pistol gently back into his bag, not willing to push the Marshal far enough to cause a physical confrontation if he didn't need to. Beneath the cool expression of this interstellar cowboy, mixed in with that intense stare and casual manner was real steel.

There were many men and women on Nix with that look in their eyes, each soul carrying the scar of madness' touch in their own way. A mere moment of eye contact, twitch of the hand, or certain tenor of voice is often enough of a warning sign for those foolish enough to cross paths with them.

The Marshal had called his bluff, and one doesn't bluff with a hard man.

Kristos knew he didn't stand a snowballs chance in Hell against this lawdog in a gunfight. Math didn't lie.

At this range there was no statistical chance he could survive a hail of zero-g micro-flechette rounds if the lawdog pulled his service revolver.

If, and only if, Kristos did manage to come out on top in a blazing battle with EnerCorp's trained killer, there would be terrible reprisals for his singular moment of luck.

A corporate crackdown would surely follow, probably in the form of a battalion of lawdogs. There would be hell to pay, each one frothing at the mouth to revenge their fallen brother.

Flourishing his hands slowly to show the pistol was gone and only his hands remained, "So, lawdog. What is it I, The Great Doctor Kristos Lamont, can do for you?"

"You know we have a problem don't you, Doctor?"

"Anyone having conversation with a lawdog who doesn't enjoy the tickle of pillow talk in the early hours of morning would seem to have a problem. But yes, I get your meaning."

Nodding his head in agreement, a small sliver of a grin showing beneath his thick ruddy mustache, Johnston leaned forward so Kristos could clearly see the seriousness not his face.

“Your little operation here, as amazing as it is, has taken the great leap feared by all men of fortune who seek their fate upon the Black.” Waxing momentarily poetic, Johnston took one last drag, before crushing the gasper out beneath his booted feet. “Your meddling and mucking about with the gears of the system have drawn the attention of The Powers That Be and the great watchmakers back in Houston do not appreciate meddlers, Doctor.”

“Is it so hard to look upon a printed page, lawdog?” Kristos was stalling, trying to give his calculating mind a chance to make the connection.

Had he been singled out of all those involved with making Nix run?

"Why would those so far away send their a shadowy gun-thug to drag me out in chains? All this for giving people hope in their time of need?"

Perhaps he wasn't singled out? Maybe he was the last.

Kristos' blood chilled at the thought of the others on the Council waiting in some hidden paddy wagon docked at one of the emergency airlocks?

Perhaps the lawdog isn't here to arrest any of us; perhaps he's here to make us all go away? It wouldn't be the first time EnerCorp made something disappear was it?

Lighting up another smoke, the acrid gasper adding a leathery rasp to Johnston's voice. The gravely ol' Marshal put it as plainly as he could, laying all his cards out on the table.

“You can have all the hope you want, Doctor. What you don't have is the permission to put people's lives in danger or rob EnerCorp of billions in valuable time, tech, and resources.”

“Now see here, lawdog,” Kristos snarled with indignation and anger, taken aback by the accusation he was putting people's lives in danger. “I never send anyone out with the idea of putting their lives in danger. The men and women who scavenge the things we need here in Nix take on the work voluntarily. Each one understanding they put their lives in harm's way for their own good as well as the good of the community-- ”

“Let's be honest, Doctor,” Johnston stepped in quickly, “Nobody cares if some random mine rat floated past Beacon One and directly into the path of a long-haul freighter on its way to Mars Dome.

Johnston sat back in the rickety old chair, taking another deep drag off the gasper, “Recycling old relics like this derelict or recovering parts from floating wrecks is one thing. Creating a mid-flight emergency just to strip their spacecraft of everything valuable is another thing entirely.

Both would have eventually drawn my attention but it's the flight crews your “people” have been putting in harm's way and that officially put you on my radar.

Johnston watched as Kristos' face went from indignation to worry at the mention of hijacking long-haul flights. “From your reaction, you have no idea what I'm talking about, do you?”

Don't ask. I don't want to know. That was the deal he made with the Council.

“You just make it work, and we will take care of the rest,” was what they had said.

Kristos had just assumed there were enough mining operations and unmanned stations in the system that they wouldn't be stupid enough to spit in the face of the corporation by robbing them mid-flight.

EnerCorp had sent the lawdog here for one reason and one reason only: sending him to fix the problem was cheaper than losing one more shipment.

Everybody's life had suddenly become forfeit because of the actions of a few simple-minded but well-intended idiots.

"I wouldn't know anything about that," Realizing he was in enough trouble, Kristos toned his rhetoric down. Ruffling this man's feathers anymore than they already were just didn't make any sense. "but since you know me so well. You must know my old rig has a corp beacon. If I was within a quarter million miles of these "incidents" there would be a record of it, Marshal."

"And that is the only reason you aren't in cuffs right now, Doctor."

From what Johnston could tell, Doctor Kristos Lamont might be the most trusted man on Nix but he wasn't getting the whole truth from those helping him.

"Ingenious, that. Converting the nitrogen ice up top with nitrogen fuel cell converters and then recycling what moisture left into usable water rain water for the gardens. And guess what... Only you could have done it.

"Only one out of a thousand of the mush heads eating at your troughs have more than a rudimentary working understanding of the sciences, and none of them have the ability to put it all of it together with what you have."

Johnston shifted in his seat and lit up another of the scraggly smokes, spitting the lose tobacco from his lips. "See that makes you responsible in any court in the entire system.

“A good corporate lawyer will argue blah blah, 'If he hadn't drawn up the plans for such an extravagant vision then his loyal followers wouldn't have taken to hanging blokes out to dry,' blah blah. So you are screwed either way. What I can't figure out is why?

“Top of your class, early entrance to the CorpCentral, top salary, top wife, a house straddling a stable stretches of beach front property on Earth. What makes a man like that just toss in the bin to play gardener for a bunch of station rats?”

Kristos sat silent, staring back at Johnston, not avoiding his glare but unable to give him an answer. How could he express to anyone what drove his flight when he didn't really understand the complex equations that obsessed his mind?

“Nothing... really?” Johnston was actually surprised by the silence. It didn't fit his personality profile or what he had witnessed in his weeks of surveillance.

“You don't want to say anything on your behalf when I'm your last shot at retaining any semblance of life in light of your current predicament? You were a genius, revered as a hero. You made life on Heliah One possible, Doctor.”

“ ‘I still believe that peace and plenty and happiness can be worked out some way. I am a fool.’ “ Kristos rubbed his hands on his face, trying desperately to hold back all that he knew; a knowledge that had driven him to the edge of madness and back..

“Vonnegut, Doctor Lamont? How about Thomas Fuller? ‘A fool's paradise is a wise man's hell.’ “

Kristos felt the damn burst inside. The wall between the world and his dark secret cracking beneath the gaze of his interrogator. If his sins were to be exposed, so be it.

But let all those who have sinned in the name of progress be impugned by the light

"You talk of heroes and greatness, as if these virtues were applicable to me in some way. I am as heroic as Paris when he steals away with Helen of Sparta, knowing the hell spurred by the rage of Menelaus would rain down suffering on his beloved Troy. I am as great as the men who thought splitting the atom could bring peace through war, Marshal."

With a wild look in his eyes, it just came out of Kristos mouth before he knew it. "Do you want to know the truth of Heliah One, Lawdog? The real truth?"

Johnston sat forward slowly, nodding his head silently. The doctor seemed to be on the verge of tears as he tried to spit out whatever was haunting his soul.

"Nine minutes fifty eight seconds into *Dunstan*'s flight, she exploded. Barely outside the rim, a massive plasma charge created by static electricity crossing the super-conducted platinum ignited the anti-hydrogen vents supplying the FTL drives."

The tears flowed freely down Kristos' face. All the death and pain he caused dripping from between his dirty fingers and onto the deck plates.

"She was ripped to pieces, all hands lost. There is no colony on Heliah One"

"Don't believe me?" The lack of impact of his confession had on the lawdog infuriated the Doctor.

"Go! Go see what we have done! You can get the nav locater off my ship. I searched for her for five years after launch, and there's nothing left of *Dunstan* but a debris field around a dying locator beacon."

Kristos' voice was strained from venting so many years of pain at once but it was like confession when he was a little boy. Once started, he couldn't stop till the darkness eating away at his soul was gone.

"The death of *Dunstan* was my fault for not standing up to Enercorp, for not telling the world there were flaws in the capture and containment units and I would like that to go on the record Marshal."

The two men sat silent for a moment as Kristos trying to regain some composure in the wake of freeing his anger, rage, and sadness. "So now you know my great secret, lawdog. The genius who never was. A hero for staying silent when lives were on the line."Pulling his long curly hair back from a tear stained face, Kristos felt free, and completely resigned to his fate. "Do what you will, lawdog. Take me back to your sound-proof cages shadowed in endless night. At least there I can go properly mad. Because if you take this away from these people, all is lost again and nothing will matter to me then."

Johnston sat back in the wobbly little office chair, a warmth spreading through his chest he hadn't felt in a long time. Pride. This man's pain, his drive to redeem himself for a sin of omission was inspiring.

After almost a lifetime of dealing with worst the system could throw at him, the grizzled ol' lawdog had finally met a good man in the darkness and that gave him hope.

"Can I ask you a question Doctor?" Johnston's baritone filling the silence between them. "Did you think you were alone in your despair?"

Kristos looked up as Johnston moved his chair closer to the good doctor. Shaking out a smoke, the Marshal handed the gasper over and lit it up as the Doctor's brought it to his slightly trembling lips.

"When you arrived at that lonely little patch of deep space, I'm assuming your proximity sensors flooded with collision alerts from the tons of debris. Correct?"

Kristos nodded his agreement. Thinking back, he was lucky to get out of the quadrant without destroying the *Versailles* in the process.

"Did you pick up an emergency distress beacon signal?" Johnston asked.

"Yes, but it was far too deep in the wreckage for me to maneuver into without putting my own ship in danger. I figured it was anomalous piece of space junk since there wasn't anything large enough out there to help anyone," Kristos replied.

"Always the smart man, Doctor. That beacon was there because that's where we left it. I was part of the reaction team on board *Atlantica* when word came down to command that there might have been a problem with the Heliah flight.

"We picked up the auto-distress call a full hour and a half before you eggheads at the Cape and the military took control. That's why you, along with everyone else in the system, were kept out of the loop, Doctor. You know the protocols: the minute lives are on the line in an inter-stellar accident the military is required to step in--"

"And the military does what the military does. It keeps things quiet," Kristos said softly, realization sud-denly coming into his mind.

"Exactly Doctor. It took us six months to track down the last known location of *Dunstan* but by then we had long since updated *Anne* on the situation. Backup vehicles using the same nuclear pulse generators were outbound less than a year after the accident and quietly everything that was lost on board of *Dunstan* was back in transit."The mission, although behind schedule and seriously hampered by the lack of anti-hydrogen flight drive, continues and someday the heroics of those men will be celebrated... just not now.

"It may not be a happy gift-wrapped life like some thought it would be, Doctor, but Heliah will live and you could have had a part of it if you hadn't abandoned everything you believed in to build this," Johnston motioned to everything around him, "And this is a problem that we now have to solve."

Both men knew what would happen to these people if they shut Nix down. They would be thousands of shapeless bundles of dirt and shambling fabric hiding in the corners of space stations from here to Mercury Prime.

It spooked Johnston to see the number of familiar faces wandering the myriad communities here on Nix; some of them he hadn't seen since before *Atlantica* went down off Neptune. Gunners, pilots, medics and cooks: these were men and women Johnston never expected to see hiding amongst the rats.

Hell, there were even a few ol' lawdogs running around below decks; a knowing wink or nod of the cap enough to identify them in a crowd. And most of them would die with no place or purpose in the universe if they shut down Nix.

Oh, yes... Enercorp would take back those healthy enough to work the belt, under limited contracts, of course. A man had choices in life, and it was up to him make the most of it.

No. He wouldn't shed a tear for the rats of Nix.

It was the children. Singular souls burning as bright as any star in all the universe. Their laughter jingled like bells in his ears while playing tag amongst the trees great gardens.

It was they who would truly suffer.

Johnston had seen it a thousand times. A twenty year contract was a life sentence for a child. They would never know another kind of life, only one of relentless work or crime. Hell, most of the adults here on Nix were bastard orphan children of those far flung outfits on the rim.

At least here they had some semblance of normality.

There was a makeshift school, with men like the Doctor strengthening their minds with knowledge that made life more than just an exercise in commerce. When they fell, there was a makeshift medical team to heal their scrapes, cuts and occasion broken bones.

But most importantly, all of them had freedom.

Freedom from the crushing pace of contract life. Their days are filled with happiness instead of twelve grueling hours trapped in a suit or 200 meters beneath the surface of massive asteroid. At night, when called home to their beds; most went off to dreamland with a bellyfull of fresh food that they didn't have to dig through hell to get.

This may not be much of home, but to people who had never walked on a planet, Nix was a paradise compared to the alternative.

Before he left Neptune Station, Johnston made *the* call to Houston. Someone higher up than he had to have an opinion on this one.

Their answer was simple, "Burn it down or leave it be. Just make the raiding stop, Marshal Kipling."

That was a damn big blank check, and Space Marshal Johnston Kipling had made up his mind to cash it.

"The way I see it, Doc. You have a law problem around these parts and it has to do with two things." Johnston made sure he had Kristos attention. What he was about to do could cost him his whole career, there was no way he was gonna' make this offer twice.

"One: you need to stop mucking about with trying to harvest power for this old derelict from sources that can never possibly support it. You are smart man; get a crew together, get down below deck and figure out how to get those reactors running. As long as the raiding stops, no one from the company will bother you when Nix comes back online."

"And the second," Kristos asked as a smile tried to creep onto his face.

“The new Sheriff of Nix Colony will keep the rats in line but you have to keep him well stocked in these,” and Johnston pulled a fresh gasper from his pocket, puffing it to life.

“What new Sheriff?”

Offering up his rough hand, his warm smile obscured by a cloud of gray smoke, “Pleased to meet you, Doc.

“The name's Johnston Kipling, at your service...”

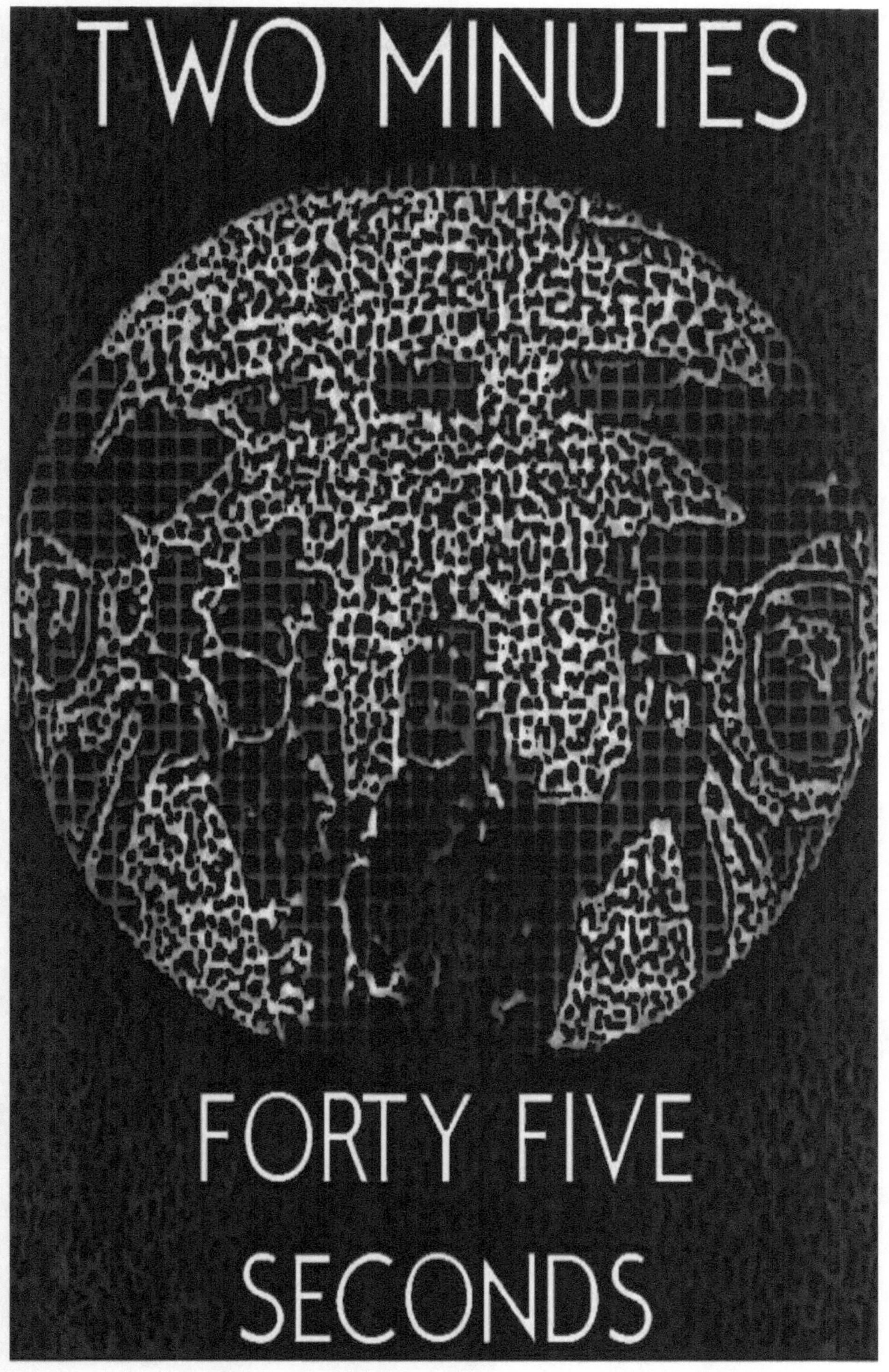
TWO MINUTES
FORTY FIVE
SECONDS

Two Minutes Forty Five Seconds

Two minutes and forty five seconds is a long time.

It is January 28, 1986, a crystalline blue day at Cape Canaveral.

Surrounded by clicking cameras and roving reporters, the family and friends of seven American heroes stand shivering together in the frigid morning breeze. A bitter, unnatural cold hung in the salty Atlantic air, but even the grip of a bleak winter morning was unable to numb their collective, nervous excitement.

Perched on the it's great orange roost, Challenger gleamed bright white under the blinding light of January's sun. Having waited days for just the right moment, the majestic bird of prey was finally ready to strike out at the void just beyond the grip of Earth.

Delay after delay, day after day, it had taken a long time to come to this moment. Scientists, musician, teacher, pilots, astronauts...heroes. Strapped in tight, our intrepid explorers waited through the endless check-lists for their moment with the stars.

Today was their day as the countdown clock strikes all zeros, the solid rocket boosters lighting moments after main engine ignition. As the ground rumbled and shook before Challenger's great leap from her roost, some probably gritted their teeth, let loose a small giggle or a nervously held breath as over three million pounds of thrust poured out of the engines.

At eleven thirty eight a.m. Challenger screamed towards the heavens and destiny.

*

They didn't know.

The high speed cameras knew. They took hundreds of pictures of every launch from up close and afar since the beginnings of the space program. In their unfeeling eye's a secret had been captured; a secret they wouldn't tell until human eyes would pour over them in the weeks, months, and years to come.

Frozen in time, moments before the bonds of gravity let loose of Challenger on the launchpad; an anomalous puff of black smoke flowed down the bottom of the right solid rocket booster, and disappeared into the confluence of smoke and fire at the base of the launchpad.

Someone in Houston and Cape Canaveral knew. Before launch engineers from Morton Thiokol warned them. They knew the dangers that morning, gas blow out concerns about the O-ring joints on the solid rocket boosters were documented as far back as Columbia's second flight.

They knew the O-rings in the Solid Rocket Boosters would become brittle and non-malleable in the thirty one degree temperatures of that frigid January morning.

And yet, despite the initial recommendation of scientific minds at Morton Thiokol, the temperature was not considered a flight hazard.

Did Washington force their hand? The Teachers in Space Project had drawn the biggest public response to the Space program in a decade. Hundreds of millions in public as well as private dollars were on the line, Washington couldn't afford a failure.

What can not be disputed....The heroes didn't know.

**

They were at the pinnacle of their glory. Riding a bone rattling, adrenaline laced flight into the heavens, all of them blissfully unaware of their coming fate.

Fifty-eight seconds into the flight that tiny plume of spewing fuel from the right solid rocket booster, leaking since lift-off, grew larger as it burned away at the aft strut holding it in place.

For ten more seconds, things inside Challenger and on the ground were green. No one imagining the damage that one tiny leak was about to unleash.

“Go at throttle up,” Capcom (Capsule Communication) in Houston calls out to its rising spacecraft.

Challenger's commander replies calmly, "Roger, go at throttle up," .

A jolt to the right shook Challenger as the starboard solid rocket booster begins to pull away from its supports. The fire melting its struts, fueled by the pressure of escaping fuel and there is nothing anyone or anything could have done to stop it.

Seventy-two seconds into the flight, the ashen-colored Solid Rocket Booster finally gives up its hold on Challenger, plunging deep into the heart of the now burning main fuel tank.

The following explosion is cataclysmic.

The last thing heard on the crew cabin intercom recorder is a simple, “Uh-oh....”

All communication was lost with Challenger as the main fuel tank detonated, leaving behind a great cloud of water vapor and burning debris. Liquid oxygen and hydrogen combine in the atmosphere; giving birth to a morbidly beautiful, blossoming, achromatic flower of death.

***

Nationwide hundreds of children watched the death of the Space Age live on television. Some polls suggest that forty eight percent of 9 to 13 old students in 1986 witnessed the launch live while the rest of the country learned within an hour of Challenger's fate.

I was one of these children.

Some teachers went out of their way that day so their students could see this moment in history, scheduling Science Fairs and presentations to coincide with the launch.

This was a moment of pride for all teachers to celebrate with their impressionable charges, when one of their own went above and beyond for all students everywhere.

Some of us cried, while others threw up on their Reeboks, and none of us really had any idea what had just happened. An entire generation of children watched as their heroes died on national television and no one knew what to say. The teachers, struggling with their own grief and shock, turned off the television sets and sent those that could go back to class.

Thinking back on it now, I am thankful that our youthful innocence shielded us from reality.

We didn't think about how much they must have suffered. In our minds, they died in an extraordinary ball of smoke and fire; an instantaneous death frozen for all eternity in darkest parts of our consciousness.

We didn't know that they tried to save themselves as the massive orange fuel tank disintegrated beneath them. Our youthful minds couldn't imagine the G-forces and wind shear tearing at the fragile airframe of Challenger. The savage pressure ripping off her wings and nose, her payload cabin exploded from the stresses like a bomb.

No one knew that the cockpit portion of Challenger had broken free virtually intact. Our heroes had survived the explosion and would live for an additional two minutes and forty five seconds.

****

Can you smell the sweat in the cabin?

Can you hear the cries of the frightened?

The growled commands of the commander and pilot as they tried to right their beleaguered, doomed spacecraft?

Did they know they were flying a giant metal box as the wind shear shredded away any recognizable airframe of Challenger?

Was there still hope as they briefly continued up and away in their trajectory from the cloud of fire? Did that hope disintegrate in the face of their Mach 2 descent, speeding at twice the speed of sound towards the gray ocean below?

Undoubtedly the flight stick would have beaten the commander mercilessly as he fought desperately to pull what was left of Challenger up and out of her dive, trying everything his mind could muster from a lifetime of flying experience.

It wouldn't have matter how much of Challenger was left. Not while his crew and craft plummeted towards the rapidly expanding blue wall coming at them at fifteen hundred miles per hour.

Two minutes and forty five seconds....

Three-time space shuttle commander and NASA Investigator *Robert Overmyer* told **NBC** news correspondent *Jay Barbree* before his death in 1996: *"They were alive...Scob fought for any and every edge to survive. He flew that ship without wings all the way down."*

Two minutes and forty five seconds is a long time when you are falling at over fifteen hundred miles per hour. Long enough perhaps to survive?

If NASA had left in the modified SR-71 Blackbird ejection seats like the original design called for might the outcome have been different?

Why wasn't the full pressure suits that were part of the compliment for the first four shuttle flights mandatory?

Do the math... Do all the ifs add up to survival?

The impact with the Atlantic at Mach 2 cataclysmically and quickly ended our heroes' lives. A merciful release compared to their terrifying tumble from the heavens.

Two minutes and forty five seconds is a long time.

You can kiss your child fifty, maybe sixty times if they don't wiggle and giggle too much in that amount of time. Fortunes have been won and lost with less time on the clock.

Dreams live and die in between the hands of a clock.

A child's dreams.... My dreams.

www.ingramcontent.com/pod-product-compliance
Lightning Source LLC
Chambersburg PA
CBHW020821180626
46814CB00001B/58

9780615977201